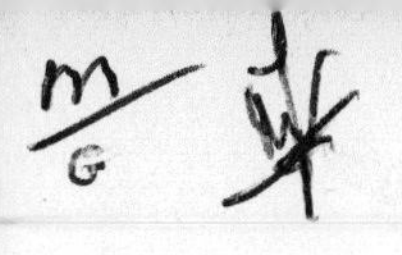

HASHKNIFE OF STORMY RIVER

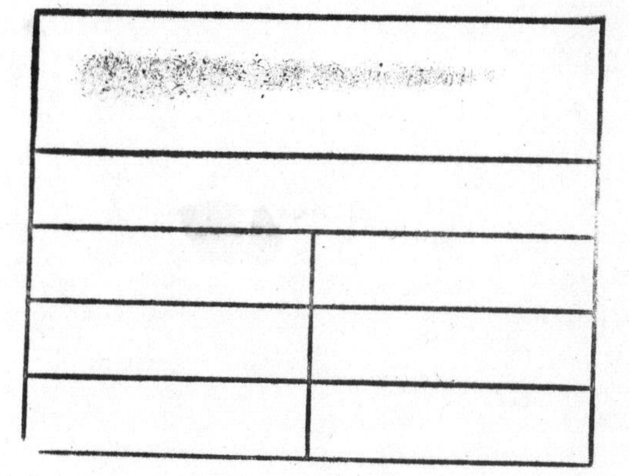

HASHKNIFE OF STORMY RIVER

W. C. TUTTLE

First published in Great Britain by Collins
First published in the United States by Houghton Mifflin

Published in Large Print 2012 by ISIS Publishing Ltd.,
7 Centremead, Osney Mead, Oxford OX2 0ES
by arrangement with
Golden West Literary Agency

British Library Cataloguing in Publication Data
Tuttle, W. C. (Wilbur C.), 1883–1969.
Hashknife of Stormy River.
1. Western stories.
2. Large type books.
I. Title
813.5'4–dc23

ISBN 978–0–7531–8999–3 (pb)

Printed and bound in Great Britain by
T. J. International Ltd., Padstow, Cornwall

CHAPTER ONE

It was early morning in the town of Pineville; so early, in fact, that there was little activity. The lamps were still burning in the Stormy River saloon, where tired-eyed cattlemen, ignoring the fact that this was Sunday morning, shuffled and dealt poker hands, drinking occasionally.

At the long hitch-rack in front of the place nodded a dozen cow horses, whose owners had forgotten them since early in the evening. A man came from the saloon, carrying two big buckets, which he proceeded to fill at a squeaky old pump, breaking the stillness of the sleeping town.

Two men were standing in front of the sheriff's office. One man was tall, thin, with a sad face; the other a small, wiry, sharp-faced man, with graying hair. The tall man was dressed in wrinkled black clothes, which did not fit well, a white shirt, polished of bosom, and an extra high stiff collar. He wore no vest, and his glaring red four-in-hand necktie gave him the appearance of a man who had had his throat cut. He leaned against a porch-post, shifting his weight from one foot to the other, as though his new boots were just a size or two too small.

"Yuh say yuh busted it all to hell, eh?" said the small man, who was Pat Lynch, the sheriff of Stormy River County.

Oscar Johnson, the black-clad deputy, nodded sadly.

"Tryin' to drive with one hand, Oscar?"

"Nossir."

"Had a girl with yuh, didn't yuh?"

"Shore. Annie Hall was with me, Pat. I was drivin' with both hands, though. I dunno. Mebby the horse flipped his tail over the lines. It was dark. First thing I knowed, he kicked the dash off the buggy, and then started runnin'.

"Busted dash didn't mean nothin'. I says fer her to set tight, and we come a-runnin'. 'Course everythin' was all right, until we hits that culvert jist outside of town, and we does a 'thank-yuh-ma'am' that jist caved in the wheels.

"But I hung to the lines, and when we lit — well, as soon as I gets untangled from Annie, I finds the horse upside down and the buggy fit fer fixin'. I gets the horse to his feet and managed to drag the buggy behind the blacksmith shop. And that's where she is now, Pat."

"Annie Hall?"

"No! The buggy. Annie went home."

"Wasn't she hurt?"

"Nothin' special. Kinda limped."

"And you in that new black suit, Oscar."

Oscar sighed deeply and looked down at himself.

"I thought of that, Pat. But there wasn't no time to make a change. I'm sorry about the buggy."

"Yuh ought to be. Cost me a hundred and sixty dollars in Cheyenne — also new — good buggy, I'll tell yuh."

"One of the best I ever smashed."

"Yuh don't need to be funny about it, Oscar."

"Think I ort to cry about it? Yo're lucky to have me back alive."

"Some folks have a damn queer idea of what constitutes luck," said the sheriff dryly.

"Oh, it wasn't all luck," blandly. 'I used m' head."

"Yea-a-ah, I'll betcha. Well, let's go over and look at the wreck. I reckon you'd like to see me git it back in the same condition it was when I loaned it to yuh, Oscar."

"Like to — yes; but it ain't hardly possible."

"I mean — I don't like to have to pay for fixin' it."

"I don't blame yuh, Pat. Won't hardly be worth it. Anyway, yuh don't need no buggy."

"Well, you was the one who busted it."

"Yuh can't argue with me — I did."

The sheriff snorted disgustedly. He didn't like to come right out and ask Oscar to pay for the fixing of the buggy, and he knew that Oscar never would do it voluntarily.

"That was a great dance at Garnet," offered Oscar, as they crossed the dusty street toward the blacksmith shop, which was near the Stormy River saloon.

"Best callin' I ever heard. My hoofs shore feel like I'd been on hard pasture for a long time. Fact of the matter is, I wouldn't know I had any feet, unless I look down at 'em, they're that numb. Good crowd too. Lotsa girls."

"Yuh ort to wear boots that fit yuh, Oscar."

"Fit? Hell, I got into 'em, didn't I?"

"You wouldn't call the skin of a sausage a perfect and comfortable fit, would yuh? Some of you cowpunchers make me sick. Ain't got brains enough to wear comfortable boots. My gosh, you'd think there was a prize offered for the most uncomfortable feet."

"There's yore buggy," said Oscar sadly, as they halted at the rear of the shop, littered with the running gears of a wrecked wagon, a wheelless cart, and all the refuse of a cow-town blacksmith shop.

"Yeah, that's my buggy," admitted the sheriff. "If it wasn't fer that yaller paint on the wheels, I'd never recognize her. You shore massaged it a plenty, Oscar."

"The top's all right, Pat."

"Yea-a-ah; and one shaft. Why didn't yuh bust off that shaft and use it to beat hell out of the top? Might as well have made it unanimous."

"I s'pose. Still, old Sam Hall is a pretty good blacksmith, and he might put her together agin'."

"Oh, yea-a-ah! Take the blacksmith's daughter to a dance and — whatcha tryin' to do — git in good with old Sam?"

"Aw, I didn't do it on purpose, Pat. 'S far as I'm concerned, I don't give a damn whether he fixes it or not."

Pat Lynch straightened up from an examination of a smashed wheel, sighed deeply and considered his deputy.

"Sometimes I damn near hate you, Oscar."

"Thasall right, Pat. Everybody is entitled to their opinion. I won't argue with yuh. Fact is, I'm too sleepy and sore to argue with you. Remember, I got drug about forty feet, with Annie on my lap. She ain't no feather piller, yuh know. Jist about ruined my new suit. I'm inclined to be sorry about the buggy, but at the same time —"

Oscar's voice trailed off to a stop, as he stared at the corner of a little corral, which enclosed a small stable behind the Stormy River saloon. The sheriff turned and gazed in the same direction.

"Whatsa matter, Oscar?" he asked.

"I dunno," Oscar spat dryly. "Feller layin' on the ground over there by the corner of the fence. Mebbe he's jist drunk, but he's in a funny position."

The sheriff stepped past Oscar, where he could get a better view.

"Too much liquor," he decided. But Oscar wasn't sure. He walked over to the corral and looked at the man.

"You better come here, Pat," he called softly. The sheriff left the wrecked buggy and came quickly.

The man was lying flat on his face, arms spread out, the fingers clutching the dirt. His hat was lying several feet away. Neither the sheriff nor the deputy spoke for several moments. The back of the man's head had been smashed in, and he was a welter of blood.

There was no use of an examination; no use in turning the body over. They both knew it was Buck Dennig, and that he was dead. Oscar reached out and braced himself against the corral fence, as he wet his dry lips with his tongue.

"Somebody's killed Buck Dennig," he said softly.

"Somebody did," nodded the sheriff. "Been dead quite a while too; prob'ly couple of hours, or more."

Oscar nodded slowly, and they considered the murder in silence.

"We ought to tell about it," suggested Oscar. He stepped farther toward the other corner, looking between the poles of the corral. On the opposite side of the corral, tied to the fence, was a tall sorrel horse.

"That's Buck's horse," said Oscar. "He mostly allus ties him back there. Said that the sorrel scares easy, and might break loose from the hitch-rack. Who do yuh suppose killed Buck?"

"This ain't no guessin' contest. C'mon."

They went back through the alley and entered the Stormy River saloon. Only one poker game was still in progress, and around the table sat "Hootie" Cooper, a merchant, Frank Shell, a gambler, Mort Heffner, prosecuting attorney, Lester Cline, another merchant, "Dobe" Severn and Bud Hough, two of the TD cowboys.

They nodded to the sheriff and deputy. Heffner yawned widely and looked at his watch, not realizing that it was already daylight.

"When did Buck Dennig leave?" asked the sheriff casually.

"About two o'clock," replied Dobe Severn sleepily. "And it's about time for us to foller suit, Bud."

"Yeah; or get me somethin' to prop my eyes open with," grunted Bud, intent on his cards.

"Well, he didn't git far," said the sheriff seriously. "He's layin' out there by the corral, with the back of his head smashed in."

The players blinked at the sheriff, hardly understanding what he had said. Heffner got slowly to his feet, his hands on the table.

"You mean that somebody killed Buck?" he asked.

"Jist that, Mort. Smashed in his head."

"Well — well —" faltered Bud vacantly, "he was all right when he left here."

"That shore sounds intelligent," grunted Oscar.

None of them waited to cash in their chips. They filed out through the rear entrance, which was only about sixty feet from where the body lay.

"Don't touch him," warned the attorney. "One of you go and get the coroner. Just let the body alone. There isn't a thing you can do now."

Dobe Severn ran down the alley, hot-footing his way after the coroner, while the rest of the men stood stiffly around the body.

"Looks pretty damn bad," said Hootie Cooper, a thin-faced, little man, with a huge nose and a squeaky voice.

"For Blanco," said Lester Cline, a much younger man than Cooper. They were business rivals in everything except kerosene. Hootie wouldn't handle it, because it had been the cause of him burning out his store at one time.

The sheriff turned his head quickly and looked at Cline.

"What about Blanco?" he asked sharply.

"That don't prove anything," said Shell, the gambler, quickly.

"No, it shore don't," agreed Cline. "But just the same —"

"What's this all about?" demanded the sheriff.

"Buck Dennig and Blanco quarrelled last night," said the gambler. "Buck just the same as accused Blanco of stealing a card. I didn't see it. Mebby Buck had been drinking."

"I didn't see it," said Hootie. "I was watchin' the play. Blanco was dealin'. Looked to me as though it was square.

"Did they fight?" asked the sheriff anxiously.

"No," said the gambler shortly.

"They was mad enough," yawned Bud. "Blanco's lips were as white as anythin' yuh ever seen. And he never turned a hair, when Buck —"

"Don't say too much," advised the gambler. "Just because two men quarrel —"

"I want the straight of this," interrupted the sheriff. "You say they didn't fight, eh? Did Blanco leave the game?"

"He did. It must have been about one o'clock. He never even stopped to cash in his chips. I've still got 'em for him — about sixty dollars' worth."

"And Buck left about an hour later, eh?"

"I looked at my watch," said Hootie. "It was a quarter of two."

Little more was said, and in a few minutes the coroner came with Dobe. The coroner was an old cow-town doctor, short of speech, familiar with everybody's ailments for a radius of twenty-five miles.

His examination of the dead man was very brief. Outside of the smashed skull, Buck Dennig had not been touched.

"One good swipe would have done it," said Hootie.

"One *good* swipe," admitted the doctor grimly. He had known Buck for a long time.

"Take him out to the ranch?" queried Dobe.

"Take him to my office," said the doctor shortly.

After they had taken the body away, the sheriff and prosecutor went back across the street to the sheriff's office, with Oscar tagging behind them.

"You better go to bed," said the sheriff. "And for the love of gosh, git that collar and shirt off!"

"All right," sighed Oscar. "I'm sorry about that buggy."

"I hoped yuh would be."

The sheriff and prosecutor sat down in the little office and looked at each other.

"What do yuh think, Mort?" asked the sheriff. The lawyer stroked his unshaven jaw. A full night session of poker did not tend to make him abnormally bright. Not that he was a tower of wisdom at any time.

"I don't know, Pat," he replied vaguely.

"You was there when they quarrelled?"

"Oh, sure."

"Any threats?"

"Hm-mm. Well, there usually is at a time like that. I don't remember just what was said. Everybody talking, you know. But Blanco was mad, and so was Buck. In fact, Buck was mad when he came there last night."

"Mad about what?"

"Oh, I don't know what was the matter with him. Buck was usually good tempered. But something was wrong. You know, there has been a bad feeling between the TD and the Blanco outfits. Nobody has ever preferred any charges, but I think it was over some alleged rustling."

"I've heard the same thing, Mort; but never from either side. Things like that leak out, yuh know. But what do yuh think? Is there enough to base an arrest on?"

"To arrest Blanco?"

"Yeah."

The attorney shook his head quickly. "Not in my opinion. Blanco may be as guilty as hell, but we can't prove it — not yet."

The sheriff sighed with relief. He didn't want the job of arresting "Tex" Blanco, owner of the B Arrow outfit.

"We may be able to gather some evidence," said the lawyer reflectively, and then yawned widely. He was a sallow-faced, angular sort, with heavily pouched eyes. He wore a celluloid collar, cut well back to give plenty of room for his adam's apple, and celluloid cuffs, with huge cameo cuff buttons.

"We may be able to," agreed the sheriff dubiously. "But it looks to me like one of them crimes that yuh can't hang on to anybody. If Blanco killed him, and keeps his mouth shut — how are yuh goin' to put the deadwood on him, Mort?"

"I dunno." Yawning again. "I guess I better go to bed."

"How did Buck quit the game?"

"Lost about fifty dollars, I think. Ho-o-o-hum-m-m! Well, I'll see you this afternoon, Pat."

He stopped in the doorway and turned to the sheriff.

"Buck had more money with him, Pat. He had a roll of bills, fastened with a rubber band. Might see if he's still got it on him."

"All right, Mort. See yuh later."

CHAPTER TWO

The Tolman-Dennig cattle outfit, known by its brand as the TD, was the biggest outfit in the Stormy River County. Cleve Tolman had been the original owner, but ten years previous to the killing of Buck Dennig, Buck had drifted into the valley, a youth of twenty-three, with a bank roll big enough, in the vernacular, to choke a horse.

Buck was not a cowboy in those days; merely a wild youth, who had come down through the country, pitting his luck against the games of chance, and landing in Pineville with more money than he knew how to handle. Cleve Tolman needed a partner, and Buck needed an investment; so they became partners, registered a new brand and proceeded to build up a big cattle business.

Buck was a likeable sort of a chap, and he soon learned the cattle game, plunging into the business with the same dash he had used in beating cold-eyed gamblers, whose ability had been nothing against his phenomenal luck.

No one knew anything of Buck's past life; nothing of his family nor where he came from. But this was no novelty in the cattle ranges. Men only told their past if it pleased them to do so; nobody asked. Buck played on the square with everybody, and that was all that was required.

Cleve Tolman was a big man physically, with the square jaw of a fighter, rather short of speech. He always seemed content to sit back and let Buck do it. Some of the men said that Cleve was lazy. He loved to gamble, but his bad luck was proverbial.

Neither Tolman nor Buck had ever married. They employed six to twenty cowboys, according to the season, and Buck had always acted as foreman. Tolman was a director on the Pineville bank and had always had a finger in the local politics, although he had never aspired to an office.

The TD ranch was located about five miles southwest of Pineville, on Lobo Creek, the buildings almost hidden away in a big grove of cottonwoods. Little money had been spent on the ranch buildings, and none for paint. The ranch-house was a rambling, one-story building, which sprawled hither and yon among the cottonwoods, as though the architect had started something he didn't know how to finish. The bunk-house was a long, low building, with a sway-back. The big stable also swayed badly along the ridge pole, as did the sheds and other buildings.

But in spite of all this, the TD was a prosperous outfit, and rather a happy-go-lucky crew, until Dobe Severn and Bud Hough rode in that morning and told them that Buck Dennig had been murdered. Cleve Tolman and Shorty Gallup were in the kitchen, getting a list of provisions from old Luke Jones, the TD cook, when the two cowboys brought the news.

Old Luke dropped a dozen eggs on his own feet, and never even looked down at them. And Luke was a thrifty cook, too.

"You ain't jokin', are yuh, Dobe?" asked Shorty hoarsely.

"I wish t' God I was, Shorty. He's dead all right. Somebody smashed in his head, and he's laid out at the coroner's office right now."

Dobe went on to explain how he had been found, and what they had done, but Tolman did not wait to hear the details, he was heading for the stable to get his horse.

"What did the sheriff say?" asked Shorty.

"What could he say? He don't know no more about it than we do."

Matt Sturgis, Alex McLean and Eddie Grimes, the rest of the cowboys, were at the stable, and got the news from Cleve Tolman; so they came up to the house, eager for more details from Dobe and Bud, while Tolman mounted his horse and rode swiftly up the road toward Pineville.

Bud and Dobe gave them plenty of details, and they were willing listeners.

"It kinda looks to me as though Blanco's cinch was kinda gettin' frayed out," said Shorty Gallup meaningly.

Shorty was about thirty-five years of age, five feet six of tough muscles, stringy, colorless hair, pale blue eyes, deeply set on each side of a crooked nose over a thin-lipped mouth. Shorty's reputation included a willingness to fight anybody or anything at any time.

His bunkie, Matt Sturgis, was a tall, thin, grimy featured cowboy, who wore his holster tied down, and said little.

"Looks thataway," he said, in response to Shorty's observation.

"Don't prove nothin'," said Eddie Grimes, who was inclined to be technical, and then added hastily: "Oh, I know how it looks, but just because they quarrelled over a poker game —"

"You worked for Blanco one time, didn't yuh?" asked Shorty.

"I shore did, Shorty. And Tex Blanco never struck me as bein' a murderer. Anyway, his punchers think he's on the square, and he's darn nice to his old woman."

"She's a funny old woman," grinned Dobe. "Sets out there on the porch, smokin' a cob pipe. Betcha she's seventy years old."

"Sixty-nine," corrected Eddie. "And she shore can cook. She thinks a lot of Tex, and the punchers like her too."

"The first thing we know, we'll be right neighborly with the B Arrow," said Shorty sarcastically. "Eddie, yuh ought to tell all this to Tolman."

"No, I don't need to do that, Shorty. Every man is entitled to his opinion, yuh know. I'm not boostin' the Blanco outfit and I ain't tryin' to prove no alibi for Tex. But he was square with me, and I'd like to bet that a lot of the stuff he's blamed for, he never done."

"Let's arise and sing hymn number thirteen," said Shorty Gallup seriously.

Eddie smiled shortly and turned away. He knew Shorty was looking for trouble, and he had no desire to carry the matter any further. Not that Eddie wasn't perfectly capable of holding his own, but he could not see where anything could be gained by fighting.

"Well, yuh shore run yore sandy on him, Shorty," laughed Sturgis, as they watched Eddie enter the bunk-house.

"Looks thataway," agreed Shorty.

"You did like hell!" snorted Luke Jones, standing in the kitchen doorway. "You jist think yuh did. Any old time Eddie Grimes backs down it's 'cause he don't want to take advantage of a smaller man."

"Go on back to yore mulligan, you old spav!" growled Shorty. "What do you know about war? You never cocked a cannon."

"War? Say, I could take a umberelly and chase a whole dang brigade of jaspers like you plumb down to the mouth of Stormy River and never lay a hair. Yo're allus lookin' fer trouble, and hopin' t' gosh yuh never find it. Some of these days somebody is goin' to saw off yore horns; and if you git comical with me, folks will point me out and say, 'There goes Luke Jones, the feller who made a hoop out of Shorty Gallup and rolled him out of the state.' "

The door slammed shut, and they heard old Luke laughing to himself. Shorty's ears were fiery red and he started for the door, but Dobe Severn blocked him.

"Don't be a fool, Shorty," he advised. "You know Luke."

"The dirty old sheep waddy!" rasped Shorty.

"Aw, I know," grinned Dobe. "He shore can git under yore hide. But he does it for fun. He couldn't whip nobody, but he shore can make yuh mad. Let him alone, Shorty."

"I suggest that we go to town," said Bud. "There won't be no work done on this ranch on Sunday, that's a cinch. And it might look better, if we went down."

"Suits me," growled Shorty. "I reckon yo're right, Bud."

Cleve Tolman found several people at the coroner's office and they greeted him with a certain sympathy. He looked at the body, asked a few perfunctory questions, and went up to see the sheriff.

He found the sheriff talking with Lester Cline and Frank Shell, the gambler. They had gone over the cause of the quarrel between Buck Dennig and Tex Blanco, and they detailed it to Tolman again.

"But there's no evidence that Tex killed him," said the sheriff.

"He was pretty mad," offered Cline. "It looked as though they might start shooting it out right there."

"Did Blanco steal a card?" asked Tolman.

"Nobody seems to know," smiled Shell. "Buck was pretty mad; so I reckon he thought Blanco stole it. Do yuh know, it seemed to me as though Buck was looking for trouble."

"What do yuh mean?" asked Tolman quickly.

"Well, sort of irritable."

"He came down early, didn't he?"

"Sure. I saw him in the middle of the afternoon."

"It wasn't a case of robbery," said the sheriff. "He had a hundred and sixty-five dollars in his pocket."

"Makes it look worse than ever for Tex Blanco."

"I'd like to notify Buck's relatives, if we knew where they are," said the sheriff. Tolman shook his head.

"He never mentioned any, Pat."

"Did Buck ever have any trouble with anybody else?"

"What do you mean?"

"Well, did he ever have a quarrel or a fight — I mean, lately?"

Tolman looked closely at the sheriff for several moments, as though wondering what had prompted the question. Then he shook his head shortly.

"No."

"Uh-huh. Well, it looks as though we was kinda up a stump. We could arrest Tex on circumstantial evidence, I reckon; but Heffner says it wouldn't do us any good."

"Probably not," said Tolman slowly. "When is the inquest?"

"Tomorrow mornin'."

"I'll be down."

Tolman walked away from the office, and the three men looked at each other curiously.

"He's a cold-blooded fish," said Shell. "I don't suppose Buck's death affects him at all. I think he knows something, Pat."

"Knows somethin'? What about, Frank?"

"Didn't you notice the look he gave you, when you asked him if Buck had had a quarrel or a fight lately?"

"You don't think Tolman knows how Buck got killed, do yuh?"

"Probably not; but your question froze him up, just the same."

"I guess we're all lookin' for somebody to suspect," said the sheriff dryly. "And there's too much talk about Tex Blanco; too much talk and too little evidence. Tex is hot-headed, and about the time he hears what's bein' said, somebody will get pistol-whipped."

"Don't yuh suppose that the TD outfit will kinda ask Tex how about it?" queried Cline.

"Prob'ly. And I'll bet I know what he'll tell 'em. But I hope they won't. There's been bad blood between 'em for a long time, and somethin' like that might touch off the fireworks. Cleve Tolman is pretty level-headed, as a rule, but he might accidentally make a fool of himself."

Shell walked over by the door and stood there looking up the street.

"The rest of the TD outfit just arrived," he said. "I guess I better go over and open up a game."

As Shell started to step off the wooden sidewalk, he looked down the street and saw Tex Blanco and Frank Judd, one of Tex's cowboys, riding up the street toward him. He hesitated for a moment, but stopped and waited for them to ride up. The sheriff and Cline came out, and Tex reined his horse over to the edge of the sidewalk. Judd rode on to the front of a store, where he dismounted.

Tex smiled pleasantly and spoke to the three men, as he dismounted. He was a trifle over six feet tall, well built, graceful. His brown eyes and olive-tinted skin showed his Spanish blood, as did his coal-black hair, slightly gray at the temples. His nose was slightly hooked and his teeth were whiter than those usually displayed in the range countries.

He wore a gray Stetson, nearly new, surmounted with a silver band of Spanish workmanship. His shirt was of blue silk and around his throat he wore a red silk handkerchief, while around his waist he wore a multi-colored sash, with the beaded ends hanging down his left hip. He wore gray trousers, tucked in the tops of his fancy-stitched, high-heel boots, and around his waist he wore a wide cartridge-belt, sagging heavily to one side from the weight of his holstered gun.

There was no denying the fact that Tex Blanco was what is generally known as a "fancy cowboy"; perhaps just a bit more picturesque than the average, but his clothes fitted him well, and those touches of aboriginal color were not glaringly noticeable.

He stepped up on the sidewalk, still holding his reins, while the tall sorrel came in close behind him. His saddle was hand-stamped and decorated in silver, which had tarnished to a soft gray.

"Well, what do yuh know, sheriff?" he queried pleasantly.

"Not very much, Tex."

The sheriff was uneasy. Across the street and a little further up the block was the Stormy River saloon hitch-rack, where all the TD horses were tied. He was afraid of what the TD outfit might do, if they discovered Tex.

Tex seemed to feel that something was wrong. He followed the sheriff's gaze, but saw only the string of horses at the hitch-rack. Shell was looking curiously at Tex.

"What's the matter with you fellers?" asked Tex bluntly.

"Yuh didn't hear about it, Tex?" asked the sheriff.

"Hear about what?"

"Somebody killed Buck Dennig last night."

Tex frowned slightly, narrowing his eyes as he looked from one to the other.

"Buck Dennig killed? Who killed him?"

"Nobody knows, Tex. I found him this mornin', out behind the Stormy River saloon, layin' almost against the little corral fence. He'd been hit on the head — from behind."

Tex's eyes swept the other side of the street, and his right thumb hooked carelessly over the top of his belt, just above his holster.

"That's shore news to me," he said slowly. "Wasn't there no clue of any kind?"

"Not a thing, Tex. He'd been dead several hours. Left the poker game about two o'clock, and was prob'ly killed on the way out to his horse. He kept it tied to the corral fence, yuh know."

"No, I didn't know," said Tex evenly.

"Well, most everybody did," said the sheriff quickly.

Tex rubbed his freshly shaven chin thoughtfully, as he looked at Shell.

"Me and Buck quarrelled last night," he said. "You was there, Frank."

"Yes, I was there, Tex."

"I didn't steal that card, Frank."

"I didn't see it, Tex. None of the rest saw it. But that's all past. I guess Buck made a mistake. He was drinking quite a lot."

"But he wasn't drunk. I suppose everybody knows about the quarrel by this time, eh?"

The sheriff turned from looking at the saloon.

"They do, Tex. Too bad it happened. Nobody accusin' you or anybody else, but I wish you'd pull out before that TD outfit see yuh. You know what I mean, Tex. They'll be drinkin', and there's always been bad blood —"

"I usually do my runnin' straight ahead, Pat," said Tex coldly.

"I know yuh do, Tex. I'm yore friend, ain't I? Do this for me. Give that wild bunch a chance to cool off. The odds are all against yuh if anythin' starts, and it will start if they run into yuh. Give 'em twenty-four hours, and they'll see things different."

"Meaning that I killed Buck Dennig, and that I better give the TD outfit a wide berth, eh?"

"Oh, Tex, have a little sense."

Tex's brown eyes flashed with resentment for several moments, but finally he laughed softly and slapped the sheriff on the shoulder.

"All right, Pat; I guess yo're right. You can tell Tolman and his gang that — no, I'll tell 'em, when the time comes up."

Judd came from the store and Tex motioned for him to come down the street. Without saying anything more, Tex mounted his sorrel, joined Judd, and they rode back the way they came. The sheriff sighed with relief and shook his head.

"I reckon I rubbed him the right way. I shore was scared he was goin' over and meet the whole gang. And he'd do it, too."

"Didn't seem so awful surprised over Buck's death," observed Cline.

"What did yuh expect him to do — faint?" asked the sheriff caustically. "How did you act when yuh heard it?"

Cline grinned sourly, but did not reply. They walked up the street to the front of a small store, where they met Guy Shearer, the cashier of the Pineville bank. Shearer was about forty years of age, stocky built, and wearing glasses. He had been with the bank for several years.

"I heard about Buck Dennig getting killed," he told the sheriff. "Wasn't it awful? Things like that are an awful shock. Any idea who did it?"

"Not an idea," said the sheriff.

"Queer, isn't it? Buck was in the bank yesterday afternoon just before closing time, but he didn't have much to say. I asked him if he was buying more cattle, but he either didn't hear me, or didn't care to answer."

The sheriff pricked up his ears quickly.

"Just what made you think he was goin' to buy cattle?"

"From the amount of money he drew, I thought —"

"How much did he draw, Shearer?"

"Ten thousand dollars. It was a lot of money to draw from a bank the size of this one, but I gave it to him."

"Ten thousand dollars?" wondered the sheriff. "Drew it on a check?"

"Certainly."

"Well, I'll be damned! Huh! That puts a new angle on it. Who knew he drew all that money?"

"I'm sure I don't know. I was alone in the bank when he drew it; so if any one else knew it, he must have told them."

"That's an awful lot of money," said Cline slowly.

"Lot of money to have somebody steal from yuh," said the sheriff. "The question is — who knew about it?"

"Well, he must have had a reason for drawing it," replied the cashier. "Somebody else must have known about it."

The sheriff nodded and went straight across the street to the Stormy River saloon, where he found the boys from the TD ranch at the bar. They had absorbed a number of drinks, and were in the right mood for anything.

"The law is among us," declared Shorty Gallup, seeing the sheriff step through the doorway. "Hyah, Paddy?"

"All right, Shorty."

Cleve Tolman was at the back of the room, talking with Mort Heffner, the prosecutor, who had only slept an hour. They came back to the front of the saloon, when they saw the sheriff, and the three men went outside together.

"You got any opinion on this, Pat?" asked Tolman.

"I have not," replied Pat firmly.

"I've been trying to convince Tolman that there isn't a bit of evidence to connect Tex Blanco with it," said Heffner.

"And I don't agree with him," said Tolman coldly. "Tex and Buck had it in for each other. They've never been friends. And you can see for yourself that it was purely a case of revenge. His money was not touched."

"And here," said the sheriff slowly, "is just where yore theory gits all shot to hell, Cleve. Yesterday afternoon Buck drawed ten thousand dollars from the bank."

Heffner whistled softly. Tolman blinked nervously and seemed unable to speak for several moments. He cleared his throat harshly.

"Ten thousand dollars," he said hoarsely. "That's a lot of money."

"A hell of a lot," agreed Heffner. "Who told you, Pat?"

"Shearer. Buck cashed his check just before the bank closed yesterday. And Buck had a hundred and sixty-five dollars in his pocket when we searched him at the coroner's office."

"How much did he lose in the poker game?" asked Tolman.

"Not over fifty dollars," replied Heffner.

"Did Tex lose very heavy?"

"I think he was ahead of the game, but he never stopped to cash his chips; he was too mad. But he'll get his money."

"Now, the question is: who knew Buck had that money?" said the sheriff. "Shearer knew, of course, but as far as he knew, Buck disposed of it right away. Anyway, Shearer ain't the kind of a person to do a thing like that. Cleve, did you know that Buck was goin' to draw that money?"

Tolman's eyes narrowed slightly, and it was at least ten seconds before he replied:

"No."

"Buck had his own bank account?"

"Yeah."

"Wasn't there a company account?" asked Heffner.

"No."

"Well," said the sheriff, "it looks as though Buck was killed for his money."

"Not necessarily," replied Tolman. "Most any man could use ten thousand dollars."

"Sure," nodded Heffner. "That's a lot of money."

"It's a funny deal," sighed the sheriff. "No evidence at all. Tolman, I hope you'll order yore men to let Blanco and his outfit alone. It'll only start trouble. Tex was in town a while ago, and heard all about it. I didn't want him to meet yore gang today; so I induced him to go back home. But he knows what everybody's thinkin'."

"He does, eh?" Tolman smiled grimly. "I reckon yuh didn't have to argue much with him to get him to pull out."

"Tex is no fool. You'll speak to the boys, Cleve?"

"Is the law goin' to lay down on the job?"

"Not by a dang sight!"

"I'll speak to 'em, Pat."

CHAPTER THREE

It was a week after the murder of Buck Dennig that Marion Evans, erstwhile of Chicago, later of Cheyenne, climbed aboard the stage at Garnet, while "Windy" March, the stage-driver, roped her trunk to the boot, and cast quizzical glances toward the back of his lone passenger.

Windy was thin of form and face, tanned to the texture of old parchment. His face was hardly classical, due to numerous and sundry encounters, and his average chew of tobacco gave him a mumpy appearance. As a dispenser of local news, Windy was an animated bulletin board, but he was just a trifle timid around the weaker sex.

He had taken one look at Marion Evans, knocked his sombrero off, when he tried to be polite, and almost swallowed the contents of his capacious mouth. She was quite the prettiest girl he had ever seen. In fact, he had never seen any girl with such a lovely complexion. The girls of the Stormy River country were tanned from the sun and wind.

And none of them had such big brown eyes, which looked steadily at you, and her clothes were different. Windy leaned against the rear wheel of the stage, and wished he didn't have to sit beside her all the way to Pineville.

But there was no way out of it. She had climbed unbidden to the driver's seat. He took plenty of time in arranging his load, but he was finally obliged to climb up beside her and drive out of town. A close observer might have noticed that Windy had failed to fill his mouth with tobacco, and that he did not anathematize his four half-broken horses.

For a mile or more they rode in silence. The sun was warm, but a breeze sent the dust cloud behind them, like a destroyer throwing a smoke screen. The road was not too bad, and the stage was well enough ballasted to make for easy riding.

"Do you have many mornings like this?" asked the girl. Windy, looking straight ahead, shook his head.

"First one I ever had," he said slowly.

"First one you ever had?"

"Mostly travel alone, ma'am. Sometimes a puncher goes to Granite and loses his bronc, yuh know, and he has to ride back with me. This stage don't pay much — not in passengers. Haul the mail, yuh know; and some freight."

"I see. What kind of a town is Pineville?"

"Oh, all right. Needs a railroad. They thought they was goin' to git a railroad, but the railroad company didn't think they was, and the railroad company built it; so they didn't let Pineville's thoughts amount to much. Mebby some day they'll extend the line over there — but I dunno what for."

"You are pretty well acquainted around here?"

"Know every sage brush by its first name, ma'am. Raised here and got m' eddication here. Could 'a' been a big cowman, I reckon, but m' tastes didn't run thataway."

"I suppose the transportation business was of more interest to you."

"Well, I — I —" Windy floundered badly. He didn't know what transportation meant, but ended weakly, "Yes, ma'am, it was."

"This country is not what one might call thickly settled," she observed a little later.

"No, it ain't, ma'am. Yo're from the city, ain't yuh?"

"Chicago. I came here from Cheyenne."

"Chicago, eh? Well, well! I was down there six years ago. Went down with a load of TD cows. Uh-h-h-huh-h-h-h! I sh'd say I did. Say, you don't happen to know a Miss Smith in Chicago, do yuh? Had yaller hair and chawed gum. No? I dunno if she's there yet or not. I took her to a show, and durin' the evenin' somebody stole my watch and my money. She was a right good-looking girl."

"No, I don't think I ever met her," smiled Marion. "Chicago is rather a large city, you know."

"You bet. Are you goin' to stay in Pineville?"

"For several months, I hope, Mr. — er —"

"Name's March, ma'am. M-a-r-c-h. Jussasame as the month. Most everybody calls me Windy."

"Windy March?"

"Shore," laughed Windy. "Sounds like bad weather, eh? Buck Dennig named me Windy. I got sore at a couple fellers one night, yuh know. Mebbe I kinda overestimated m'self. Anyway, I went into the Stormy River saloon, intendin' to knock the whey out of 'em. I reckon I announced m' intentions; so that all might gather around and see the fun.

"Well, it didn't happen jist the way I planned. Yuh see, them two waddies jist nacherally knocked the tar out of me. They seemed to have a lot of fightin' that had to be done, and they shore worked me over a plenty. And when it was all over, I went out on m' hands and knees, plumb meek and lowly. "That's how I got my name, ma'am."

"But I don't quite understand," laughed Marion.

"Don'tcha? Buck Dennig said that March came in like a lion and went out like a lamb; so they shortened it to Windy."

"Oh, I see."

"Yes'm, that's how it comes."

"I am Miss Evans — Marion Evans. And unless something unforeseen happens, I shall teach the Pineville school this coming term."

"Well, what do yuh know about that? A school ma'am, eh? Well, yuh don't look it, and that's a fact."

"This will be my first school," she confessed.

"Well, that accounts for it, I suppose."

Windy slammed on the brake and paid close attention to his driving, until they left the short grades and entered the flat country again.

"Accounts for what?" asked Marion. Windy squinted against the sun, trying to recall what he had said.

"Oh, yeah. I done forgot for a minute. Well, I meant that they don't stay so pretty after they teach school for a long time. I reckon it kinda takes all the pretty out of 'em. It's shore a job — learnin' kids. I know they had a job learnin' me. But they stuck to it, and I came out of it all right. Takes patience, I reckon."

"I suppose," smiled Marion. "It will be a new experience for me. But one must work."

"Yeah — sure."

"I feel that I was very fortunate to be accepted by the Pineville School Board. I applied from Cheyenne, and they accepted immediately."

"Prob'ly had to have *somebody*."

Marion wanted to laugh, but she realized that there might be much truth in what Windy had said.

"I do not suppose that they are flooded with applications," she said.

"Flooded? My God! Excuse m' language, ma'am. No, I reckon nobody has ever had to set along the road with a loaded Winchester to keep the teachers out of Pineville. The last one we had almost died on us."

"Almost died on you?"

"Uh-huh. There's the Blanco ranch ahead of us, ma'am. It's a good-sized outfit. Tex Blanco owns it. We've got to stop there and drop off a package for Tex. I dunno what's in it, but it's from the Colt Company; so I don't have to be no mind reader to know it's six-shooters."

"What is a six-shooter?" she asked.

"You don't know? Well, what do yuh know about that? A six-gun is a — a hawg-leg — aw, you know — a revolver."

"Yes, I know what a revolver is."

"Well, that's them."
"I notice you carry one, Mr. March."
"Everybody does around here. Puncher without a gun is plumb naked."
"But they don't shoot each other, do they?"
"Not reg'larly, ma'am. It ain't what you'd call a common occurrence. In fact, it don't happen often enough to make it pop'lar. We wear 'em to prevent trouble."
As they drove up to the big gate, Tex Blanco, astride his tall sorrel, was just coming out.
"Got a package for yuh, Tex," said Windy. He handed the lines to Marion and stepped down over the wheel.
"All right, Windy," replied Tex, his eyes on Marion. His steady gaze caused her to turn her head, and he said softly:
"Oh, I beg yore pardon, ma'am."
"Two bits charged," informed Windy, producing the package.
Tex paid him and Windy climbed back to the seat.
"Oh, I plumb forgot." He laughed. "Miss Evans, I'd like to make yuh used to Tex Blanco. Tex, this is Miss Evans, who is goin' to teach the school at Pineville."
"I'm pleased to meet yuh, Miss Evans," said Tex slowly.
"Thank you," said Marion.
"I'll betcha yu're sorry yuh ain't got no kids to send to school, Tex," laughed Windy.
Marion flushed slightly, but did not look at Tex, who said:
"I never thought of that."

Windy spoke to the team, kicked off the brake and they went away in a cloud of dust, while Tex sat there on his horse, the package on the pommel of his saddle, until they disappeared into the hills.

"Nice lookin' feller," said Windy.

"Seemed very pleasant," replied Marion.

"He'd be jist that pleasant if he was goin' to shoot yuh full of holes, ma'am."

"Good gracious!"

"Good shot, too. Nobody paws him around. I feel kinda sorry for Tex. Lotsa folks think he murdered Buck Dennig. Mebby he did. 'Course, they can't prove it. The coroner's jury said somebody unknown killed Buck; but jist the same they all felt that Tex done it.

"There's bad feelin' between the TD outfit and Tex. The TD outfit belonged to Cleve Tolman and Buck Dennig, yuh see. Everybody liked Buck. I reckon somebody will git hurt before it's all over."

"I am sure Mr. Blanco does not look like a murderer," said Marion.

"Didja ever see one that did, ma'am? They most all look like ordinary folks, until they git convicted, and then everybody says they've got the face of a murderer. No, I can't say that Tex looks like a killer."

For the next mile or so Windy devoted himself to driving, as the road was bad along here. Once more they reached the long slope which led down toward Stormy River, and Windy relaxed.

"You spoke about the last teacher nearly dying," reminded Marion, opening the conversation again.

"Oh, yeah. But he didn't die. Kinda funny, too. The school house ain't so very big, ma'am. There's quite a few kinda big boys goin' to school, and a couple of them got so they hated the teacher; so they framed a job on him.

"At the back of the school house is a hole big enough for a man to crawl under, and at the front, under the steps, is another hole, not so big. Well, the kids got to playin' around under there, and the teacher ordered 'em to keep out from under there, cause they might crawl over a rattler.

"Well, a couple of the big boys kinda hung around after school one night, and one of 'em went in and told the teacher that a little kid had got under there and couldn't git out. He led the teacher around to the hole at the back, while the other big kid stayed under the steps and cried through the other opening.

"The teacher tried to talk with the cryin' kid, but the kid wouldn't do nothin' but talk; so he crawled under to git the kid, and these two big boys blocked the two holes. They piled cord-wood against the holes, shuttin' the blame place up tight.

"Next mornin' there wasn't no teacher and no bell rang; so everybody thought the teacher had jumped the job. And by golly, it was two days later before anybody found him."

"What a terrible thing to do!" exclaimed Marion. "What did they do to the two big boys who perpetrated such a thing?"

"I ain't sure, but I think they got dispelled."

"Literally, I hope," laughed Marion.

"I ain't sure about that," said Windy seriously.

They drove through the Stormy River crossing, where the water barely reached the hubs of the wheels. It was nearly the middle of September, and in a couple of more months there would be plenty of snow and cold weather in the Stormy River valley.

Cattle were trailing along the bank of the river, and Windy pointed out the different brands.

"There's some TD's," he told her. "Biggest outfit in the valley. I reckon it all belogs to Cleve Tolman now. Buck didn't have no folks."

"Buck was the man they think was killed by Mr. Blanco?"

"Yes'm — murdered. Prob'ly killed for his money."

"Did he have lots of money?"

"Y'betcha. Had ten thousand on him, they say."

"Gracious! Isn't that a lot of money to be carrying around?"

"I've heard that it was, ma'am; but I never had no personal knock-down to that much cash. After it gets over forty dollars, it all looks alike to me."

"I guess I know how you feel," sighed Marion. Windy shot a sideway glance at her. Windy was not so dumb he did not understand that his fair passenger was not overly burdened with worldly wealth.

"Oh, I've got a few dollars salted away," he told her confidentially.

"It must be a comfortable feeling, Mr. March."

"Mm-m-m-m."

Windy had the magnificent sum of eight-three dollars in the Pineville bank.

"Well, there's Pineville ahead of us, ma'am," he said. "That's her skyline yuh can see. Looks like a set of bad teeth, don't it? See them two molars in the middle. Them's the Pineville bank and the Stormy River saloon; two of the big business places. And they've got false fronts."

"Do you know Mr. James Lawrence Cooper?"

"James Lawrence — oh, yea-a-ah. "That's Hootie Cooper. Runs a store in Pineville. Yeah, I shore know Hootie."

"I am to board at his home — board and room."

"That's fine. Mrs. Cooper is a great big fat woman. Awful nice woman too. You'll like her fine. Good cook. Tell her she's gettin' thin, and she'll love yuh. But she ain't. If anythin', she's gettin' fatter."

"Have they any children?"

"Didn't have last Friday."

Marion laughed outright.

"Well, that's the truth," said Windy seriously. "I never lie to a lady. If it came to a showdown, I'd bet they ain't, but I wouldn't make no definite statement."

"I am just a little afraid of the board of trustees," admitted Marion. "I am not so sure of my ability, you see."

"Well, you jist forget that, ma'am. There's Hootie and old Sam Hall and Hennery Goff. That's the trustees."

"Mr. Cooper said they would investigate my qualifications, but he felt sure I would do. They will probably ask me to pass an examination."

"*They* will? Lemme tell yuh somethin', ma'am. If them three old pelicans make you pass a examination, they better ask you to write out the answer of the questions they're goin' to ask yuh — or they'll never know whether yo're right or wrong."

They drove in on the main street, and Windy drew up in front of Hootie Cooper's general merchandise store, with a squeal of the brakes, the jingle of trace chains. Hootie was in the doorway, and he came slowly out to the stage.

"Hootie, this here is Miss Evans, the new teacher," said Windy grandly.

"Well, howdy!" exclaimed Hootie. "Gosh darn! C'mon right down, ma'am."

He turned around toward the doorway, cupped his hands around his mouth, and bellowed:

"Ma-a-a-a-a! C'mere, Ma-a-a-a!"

A portly figure, dressed in printed calico, darkened the doorway, carrying her arms full of packages. Her face beamed like a full moon.

"Ma, this is Miss Evans," said Hootie excitedly.

"Well, bless your heart," panted Mrs. Cooper. She dropped the bundles and advanced on Marion, holding out her hands.

"My Gawd!" exploded Hootie. "A dozen aigs busted. There's yore omelette on the sidewalk, woman; omelette and sugar and oatmeal. Turn yore team around, Windy; here's their dinner."

But Mrs. Cooper paid no attention to her scattered groceries.

"Oh, I'm so glad to see yuh," she panted. "I told Hootie I hoped you'd be young and good lookin'. We've shore been fed up on men teachers and homely wimmin' ones. You shore do look nice. Hootie" — she turned to her husband — "you'll have to set on the porch with a Winchester and keep the cowpunchers away."

"Looks thataway," grinned Hootie.

"Well, drive around to my house and take off that trunk, Windy," she ordered. "Yuh didn't think the lady was goin' to pack it down there in her hand, did yuh?"

"Well, shore I'll take it down, Mrs. Cooper. My, my! Yo're a lot thinner than yuh was last Friday."

"I am! Last Friday I weighed two hundred and forty; today I barely tipped the beam at two hundred and forty-four — you liar."

Windy skipped up over the wheel and landed in the seat, where he kicked off the brake and headed for the Cooper home. Marion laughed with Mrs. Cooper.

"Well, thata's that," sighed the fat lady. "Hootie, put me up another order, will yuh? No, never mind. Bring it down when yuh come to dinner. I've got to talk with Miss Evans, and I need both arms. What did yuh say yore first name was? No, that's right, yuh didn't. Marion? Say, that's pretty. Mine's Gladys. But call me Ma Cooper. I shucked Gladys when I got over a hundred and seventy-five. Kinda outgrew it.

"I suppose Windy told yuh all about everybody, didn't he? Oh, he would. When he tells yuh anythin' — strain it through a sieve. He can git himself all excited over one of his own lies. But he's all right, Windy is. His heart is in the right place. Yo're from Chicago, ain't yuh? That's what Hootie told me. I've heard a lot about Chicago from Windy. He met a girl named Smith."

"He told me about her," laughed Marion, as they walked down the street.

"He would. Say, you ain't aimin' to marry a cow-puncher, are yuh, Marion?"

"Good gracious — no! What ever put that notion in your head, Ma Cooper?"

"Are yuh plumb agin' the notion of marryin'?"

"Well, I'm certainly not thinking about such a thing."

"That's all I wanted to know. As soon as some of these punchers around here see you, there's goin' to be a lot of punchers accidentally droppin' in at my place; and I want a talkin' point."

"Don't they think of anything but marriage?"

"They won't — not when they see you. I hope you'll like Pineville. It's a rough, tough place, my dear; but we don't have to lock our doors. This is my house. Them's what is left of my twelve rose bushes. Soil ain't so good. Hootie calls 'em the twelve apostles. A cow ate Matthew, Mark, Luke and John the first night they was set out. C'mon in and be at home."

"I just love it," sighed Marion. "Every one is so kind and so pleasant, I could just cry."

"Go ahead. Tears don't hurt nobody. Half a glass of water will put all the moisture back in yore system."

Windy met them at the door.

"I carried the trunk upstairs, Mrs. Cooper," he said.

"That's fine, Windy."

"Thank you, Mr. March," said Marion sweetly.

"Yo're shore welcome, ma'am."

He hurried through the gate and out to his team. Mrs. Cooper shook her head sadly.

"He's plumb ruined," she said sadly. "Roped and hawg-tied. That's the first trunk he ever carried further than the front porch in his whole life."

"I tell yuh this TD outfit is goin' to the dawgs," declared Luke Jones, as he served a belated dinner to Eddie Grimes and Bud Hough.

"What's eatin' you, Luke?" queried Eddie, eyeing a fork suspiciously. "Hey! Why don'tcha dash the soap off these implements once in a while? I got a whole chunk of soap in my mouth."

"Little soap won't hurt yuh. You'd think it was strychnine! Nobody told yuh to swaller it, did they?"

"Well, yuh ought to clean things better than that, Luke."

"Why is this outfit goin' to the dogs?" asked Bud.

"'Cause why?" Luke struck a belligerent attitude, punctuating his statement with sword-like jabs of a long-tined fork. "'Cause Cleve Tolman appointed Shorty Gallup foreman this mornin' — that's why."

"Aw, he didn't do that!" exclaimed Eddie.

"The hell he didn't! I tell yuh he did. You two was gone, when Cleve called the gang together and made the announcement. Shorty swelled up like a pizened pup."

Eddie smiled faintly and shook his head, as he helped himself to some baked beans.

"Aw, I suppose Shorty will make a good foreman," he said.

"If yuh say 'yes' to him all the time," admitted Bud.

"Well, by Gawd, here's one who won't say it to him," declared Luke. "Me and him never did hitch, and if he tries to give me any orders, this here TD will be short a cook and a foreman, 'cause he'll be runnin' to beat hell, with me after him."

Eddie laughed at Luke's serious statement.

"Don't rub him wrong, Luke. We like you and yore cookin' so well we don't want to lose yuh. Anyway, Cleve won't let him interfere with the kitchen."

"By golly, he better not. I'm strong for peace, but when I've got any fightin' to do, I do it right now. Shorty don't like me."

"You speak to Cleve," advised Bud. "Jist tell him to have Shorty lay off yore end of the job."

"Lotsa good that would do me. If Cleve ain't got no more brains than to make Shorty foreman — talkin' wouldn't do me any good. I liked Buck Dennig. By grab, he knowed how to run this ranch."

"He shore did," said Eddie thoughtfully. "We lost a good man, when we lost Buck. I wonder if Tex Blanco had anythin' to do with it. I hate to believe he did."

"I'd hate to say one way or the other," replied Luke. "Mebby it's best to let her lie the way she is. Ain't nothin' goin' to bring Buck back, and the money — well, it was Buck's own money, and he don't need it now."

Eddie looked closely at Luke, his blue eyes quizzical.

"Just *what* do you know about it, Luke?" he asked.

"I don't *know* anythin'."

Luke turned back to the store and began cleaning up the dishes, while Eddie rolled a cigarette.

"Where's the new foreman?" asked Bud.

Luke shook his head violently. "I dunno, Bud. Prob'ly gone to Pineville to get a hat that'll fit him. I was just thinkin' that it won't be so nice for you, Eddie."

"It's all right with me," smiled Eddie. "I'm just a common puncher, and I ain't wedded to no job."

"Well, don't let him run yuh off."

Eddie laughed and got up from the table. "Forty a month ain't worth fightin' over, Luke. But I think Cleve will have somethin' to say about it."

"Yo're leanin' on a damn weak reed," said Luke.

Shorty Gallup celebrated his new job by going to town with Cleve Tolman. Cleve had business with a lawyer; so Shorty centred his attentions on the Stormy River saloon, where he found Frank Judd, from Blanco's ranch, talking with Oscar Johnson and Windy March. Frank Judd was Tex Blanco's right-hand man. He was about Shorty's height, but weighed a few pounds less.

"Hyah, Shorty," greeted Windy. "Have a shot?"

"Mebby," said Shorty, looking sharply at Frank.

"How's the TD these days?" asked Oscar expansively. He had imbibed considerable liquor and was looking upon a rose-colored world.

"Pretty good," grinned Shorty. "I'm foreman now."

"You are?" exploded Windy. "Whatscha know about that? Are they goin' to quit raisin' cattle?"

Shorty didn't appreciate the humor of Windy's question, but passed it off, with a forced grin.

"I suppose," drawled Oscar, "we'll see some big changes in things around the TD."

"Yuh might," grunted Shorty. "F'r instance, there might be less rustlin' goin' on."

"Oh, is that so?" queried Windy. "Kinda reformin', eh?"

"You go to hell!" snapped Shorty. "You know what I meant."

He looked straight at Frank Judd, as he finished his sentence.

"Was you speakin' to me?" asked Frank coldly.

"If the shoe fits yuh — wear it, Judd."

"It don't fit me, Gallup. Nor it don't fit any of the B Arrow outfit."

"Is that so?"

"Yeah, that's so!"

Frank swayed away from the bar, facing Shorty, and Oscar stepped quickly between them.

"Go easy," he warned them. "Keep yore hand away from yore gun, Shorty. No use killin' each other. Yuh ort to be ashamed of yourselves."

"I'll knock his dang head off!" growled Shorty. "I don't need any gun."

"Then give it to me."

Reluctantly Shorty drew out his gun and gave it to the deputy, who turned and accepted Frank's gun. He shoved both of them inside the waistband of his overalls.

Then he stepped from between them, and without any warning Shorty rushed at Frank, slamming him against the bar, smashing at him with his free hand.

It was so unexpected that Frank had no chance to defend himself for several moments, but Shorty's blows were too wild to do more than bounce off Frank's head. Then they clinched and staggered to the middle of the room.

Shorty was mouthing curses, wearing himself out, trying to hammer Frank down with a volley of blows to the elbows and shoulders, while the cooler Frank took plenty of time to adjust himself for the work at hand.

Suddenly he lashed out with a straight right, which caused Shorty to part with two front teeth. It almost floored the new foreman of the TD. But Shorty was game. He came back with a rush, both arms working like pistons, and Frank broke ground, letting Shorty do all the fighting. But as soon as Shorty's flurry was over, and before he realized that he had done little damage, Frank's left hook caught him flush on the right ear, knocking him to his knees.

Frank stepped back, playing the game on the square, and Shorty should have stayed down long enough to allow the shower of stars to disappear; but he sprang back to his feet, still dazed, and rushed in again. But this time Frank did not retreat. In fact, he came ahead, smashing with both hands, sharp shooting at Shorty's jaw. It was all over in a moment.

Shorty was sprawled half under a card table, flat on his back, while Frank leaned against the bar, breathing heavily, unmarked, except for a skinned elbow.

"Lasted jist one round," said Windy disgustedly. "I thought it was goin' to be a fight."

"Lasted long enough to suit me," panted Frank.

"Aw, you can whip him any day in the week," assured Windy.

"That's danged little satisfaction, Windy. I didn't want to fight him."

"Well, yuh whipped him, didn't yuh?"

"I suppose that's what you'd call it."

"It shore looked thataway to me," grinned Oscar. "Mebby we better sluice him with some cold water."

Cleve Tolman didn't find the lawyer at his office; so he went on down to Cooper's store. Marion was there with Mrs. Cooper, and Hootie hurried to introduce them.

"I heard you was here," said Tolman. "One of the boys said that the new teacher had arrived."

"Yes, I arrived yesterday," smiled Marion.

Tolman frowned slightly, as he looked at her. It was on the tip of his tongue to ask her if he hadn't met her before. There was a great resemblance to some one he had known.

"Yo're a stranger in this part of the country?" he asked.

"Yes. I came from Chicago to Cheyenne, where I learned about this position. It was my first time west of Chicago."

"I hope you'll like it here, Miss Evans. It's a little rough, of course, but you'll get used to it."

"Well, we're going to make her like it," laughed Mrs. Cooper. Tolman nodded quickly and glanced toward the doorway as Tex Blanco came in. He was wearing a pair of wide, bat-wing chaps, flashing with silver conchos, and now he wore a vermilion-colored silk shirt and a blue handkerchief. He flashed a smile at Marion, as he removed his gray sombrero, and walked past them to the rear of the store.

Marion's eyes followed him, and Tolman scowled darkly. Mrs. Cooper smiled softly, and Marion flushed slightly as she turned back and saw them looking at her. Mrs. Cooper had told Marion all about the murder of Buck Dennig, and the suspicions against Tex Blanco.

CHAPTER FOUR

For several moments none of them spoke. They could hear Tex giving an order to Hootie at the rear of the store.

"Yuh better put in about four boxes of forty-fives," they heard Tex saying. "I got them new guns yesterday, Hootie; pearl handles and all. I dunno whether I'm goin' to like 'em — but they're shore pretty."

"Pretty!" snorted Tolman, beneath his breath.

"He shore loves pretty clothes and things," whispered Mrs. Cooper. "Sends to Cheyenne and has his shirts made to order."

"Hummin' bird!" said Tolman.

"Scarlet tanager," said Marion smiling.

A cowboy came across the wooden sidewalk, rasping his spurs, and struck the side of the doorway with his shoulder, as he came in. It was Shorty Gallup, his wet hair still dripping water down his face, and mixing with trickles of blood from each side of his mouth.

He stopped between them and the doorway, looking at Cleve Tolman.

"Lemme have yore gun, will yuh, Cleve?" he asked thickly, trying to talk without opening his mouth very far. His own holster hung empty on his right thigh.

"Let yuh have my gun?" queried Tolman. "What's wrong, Shorty?"

Shorty's eyes blazed as he saw Tex Blanco, who came from the rear of the store and was looking at him.

"Johnson took m' gun away from me," said Shorty, and his voice shook with anger.

"Took yore gun away from yuh?"

"Yeah, the dirty pup! And then Frank Judd smashed me in the mouth. Gimme a gun, Cleve; I want to go back."

"Take it easy," said Tolman. "Why did Frank Judd hit yuh?"

Shorty wiped his lips with the back of his hand. He was both mad and hurt, and when he glanced at Tex, who was leaning lazily against the counter, a half-smile on his face, Shorty almost exploded.

"Gimme a gun, Cleve," he begged. "Gimme a chance to clean up that damn B Arrow outfit."

Marion glanced at Tex, and their glances met. He was still smiling. Tolman stepped over to Shorty and led him outside, where they stood together, while Shorty showed him where Frank had removed two of his teeth. Mrs. Cooper sighed deeply and shook her head.

"It looks t' me as though Shorty had found somebody he couldn't whip," observed Hootie.

"It may do him a lot of good," said Tex seriously. "They are about the same size, and I'm shore Frank didn't hit him first. It's too bad this happened in front of Miss Evans. It gives her a bad impression of things."

"I'm sure it doesn't bother me in the least, Mr. Blanco."

"Well, that's fine. You'll get along out here."

"Thank you."

"Here comes Frank and Oscar," said Hootie.

The two men came across from the saloon and stepped up on the sidewalk near Tolman and Shorty. Oscar handed Tolman Shorty's gun.

"Yuh better keep this until yore foreman cools off, Cleve."

"Kinda takin' things in yore own hands, ain't yuh?" asked Tolman coldly.

"Would yuh rather have him dead than alive, Cleve?"

"By God, I can take care of myself!" rasped Shorty.

"The evidence is all agin' yuh, cowboy," grinned Oscar.

Frank Judd said nothing. His holster was still empty.

"Who started this trouble?" asked Tolman.

"Shorty did," said Oscar quickly. "He started the conversational fight, and then he started the fist fight. And he shore got what he asked for. He jist the same as accused Frank of bein' a rustler."

Tolman laughed shortly, turned and handed Shorty his gun. And almost at the same instant, Oscar jerked out the other gun and handed it to Frank, who dropped it in his holster, without looking at Shorty.

Tex stepped quickly to the doorway. His smile was gone now. He shot a glance at Frank, but centred his attention on Tolman and Shorty. The foreman held the gun in his right hand, gripping it tightly, but he was looking at Tex now.

Slowly he lifted the gun and socked it down in his holster. He was mad enough to bite a rattler, but he did not care to start trouble with Tex Blanco.

"Well, that's over," sighed Oscar.

"You jist think it is," growled Shorty.

"I guess you better go with me," said Tolman. "At least, you'll get an even break, Shorty."

They turned and went up the street together. Blanco smiled at Judd, who acted rather sheepish over the whole matter.

"He got an even break, didn't he, Frank?" asked Tex.

"Little better than an even break," said Frank.

"And a whole lot better!" snorted Oscar. "Shorty hit a dozen times before Frank hit once."

"I don't think that Mr. Tolman should 'a' taken Shorty's part in somethin' that was his own fault," declared Mrs. Cooper.

"Well, he's one of Tolman's men," said Tex slowly. "Yuh got to stick with yore own men, Mrs. Cooper."

"I thought it was goin' to mean some shootin'," said Hootie. "Shorty was goshawful mad, I'll tell yuh. He was mad at you too, Tex."

"Naturally," smiled Tex. He lifted his hat to Marion and Mrs. Cooper. "I'm shore sorry this happened in front of you ladies, and I'm glad it didn't go any further. Pleased to have met you again, Miss Evans. C'mon, Frank."

They went down the sidewalk together to the next hitching post, where they mounted and rode away.

"Tex is allus like that," said Oscar. "Nothin' ever ruffles his feathers. I reckon it's cause he ain't scared of nobody. A feller's got to have nerve to wear colors like Tex does."

"They are very becoming," said Marion. "He looks well in red and all that silver."

"But he ain't tryin' to be no dude," declared Oscar. "His father was a Spaniard and his mother was Irish. Didn't yuh ever hear her talk, Hootie? She's Irish, yuh betcha. And Tex can sling Spanish like a greaser."

"Do you suppose there will be trouble between him and Mr. Tolman?" asked Marion.

"*Is* trouble," corrected Hootie. "The TD swear that — well, no, they don't swear it, but they shore hint that Blanco and his men are stealin' TD cattle. That's what started the trouble today, wasn't it, Oscar?"

"Shore — same old complaint."

"Why don't they settle it in the courts?"

Oscar looked at her thoughtfully. "Yo're new to this here country, ma'am. Rustlin' is somethin' that ain't exactly on the law books of this country. Most cases are handled by the coroner."

"Do you suppose Mr. Blanco knows how every one feels toward him?" asked Marion. "It must be terrible to know that every one thinks him a murderer.

"It don't seem to bother him," said Oscar. "Tex is pretty salty, ma'am. He had a reputation as a killer, down in the Panhandle country. Got three men down in that country, they say. Folks kinda side-step Tex up here. He downed a gunman over in Garnet two years ago, and they tell me it was the fastest piece of gun-play yuh ever seen.

"But he never picks a fight. Takes a drink once in a while, but never more than a couple. Shorty Gallup was achin' to take a pop at Tex a while ago; but he was afraid. Even with the gun in his hand, he was scared."

"It looked to me as though Tolman was sort of givin' Shorty a chance to start somethin'," said Hootie slowly. "He shore took a chance, handin' Shorty the gun thataway. And then you hands the other gun to Judd, Oscar. You'd 'a' felt kinda mean, if they'd started throwin' lead into each other."

"Yea-a-ah; and I'd have been plumb mystified too," said Oscar slowly. "Yuh see, I took the shells out of them guns over in the saloon. I wasn't takin' no chances."

The Pineville school opened the following Monday. The trustees had hired a swamper from the Stormy River saloon to clean up the place, but it was far from Marion's idea of what a school house should be. It was a one-story frame building, thirty feet long by twenty-five feet wide, rough lumber walls, with a blackboard across the end wall.

The home-made seats were large enough to accommodate two pupils, with a two-by-six separating them. The teacher occupied an old weather-beaten desk on a slightly raised platform, which gave her a teacher's-eye view of the whole room. The walls were undecorated, except for an old clock, which refused to run longer than an hour at a time.

The board of trustees did not require Marion to pass an examination. They were only too glad to hire her. Sam Hall, the blacksmith, who talked through his nose, wanted to have an examination, but the other two vetoed such a thing.

"Well, it's all right," said Sam. "I jist wanted to ask her a problem in arithmetic to see how fast she is."

"What is it," asked Hootie.

"There's a room with eight corners in it, Hootie. In each corner sets a cat, and each cat is lookin' at seven cats. How many cats in the room?"

Hootie took a pencil and figured laboriously.

"Four hundred and forty-eight cats, Sam."

"Yo're crazy."

"I'm not. There's eight cats, ain't there? One cat sees seven cats, and seven times eight is — no-o-o, that ain't right. Each cat sees —"

"I've got it!" exclaimed Henry Goff. "Each cat sees seven cats. That makes eight cats, don't it? And there's eight cats, all seein' the same. Eight times eight is ninety-six."

"Seventy-two," corrected Hootie.

"That's right."

"I dunno," said Sam dubiously. "I've heard so danged many answers that I'm kinda confused."

"Seventy-two is the answer," insisted Goff.

"Ye-e-es and no," said Sam diplomatically. "Yo're part wrong and part right, Hennery. I'll tell yuh what let's do; we'll go up to the school house and have her work it on the board. I'd like to git it straight myself."

"All right," agreed Goff. "I'd like to prove my figures. It's twenty minutes yet before the school bell rings."

And while the board of trustees, bringing their weighty question, were preparing to advance, Marion was meeting the young ideas of Pineville and the Stormy River range.

They came on horseback, on foot, in wagons, until at least forty of them invaded the little school house. And they were of all ages, from big lumbering, sixteen-year old boys to six-year olds, attending for the first time. Lunch pails were stacked along the window ledges. The big boys eyed the teacher speculatively, wondering just how strict she might be, and talked loudly, as though trying to attract her attention to them.

But Marion paid no attention to the individual. It was as new to her as it was to many of them. Suddenly the room was hushed, and then she heard one of the big boys say:

"What do yuh suppose Tex Blanco wants here?"

Marion walked to the front of the room and stepped outside. Tex Blanco had ridden up close to the porch, carrying a little boy in front of him on that big saddle.

Tex slowly removed his hat, a smile on his lips.

"Mornin', ma'am," he said slowly, and, leaning over, he gently deposited the wide-eyed youngster on the porch beside Marion. The little, freckled-faced boy looked up at her, his blue eyes very serious.

"Yuh remember Windy March sayin' that I was probably sorry I didn't have a kid to send to yore school?" asked Tex slowly, his eyes on Marion.

"I remember it," she said.

"Well, I brought one, ma'am. Now, I ain't sorry."

"This is — is not your boy, Mr. Blanco?"

"No, ma'am. His name's Jimmy Hastings. He belongs to one of my men. His ma died a couple years ago, yuh see. Jimmy ain't never been to school before."

"But why didn't his father bring him?" asked Marion severely. "It is the duty of a parent, you know."

"Thasso."

"I — I want to know the parents, you see," she said rather lamely.

"Well, I'm sorry he ain't mine, ma'am."

"His father was busy, I suppose."

"Nope; unlucky."

"What do you mean, Mr. Blanco?"

"Yuh see, ma'am" — Tex leaned forward, resting an elbow on his saddle horn — "me and Hastings gambled on it. I put up fifty dollars against the kid, yuh might say. If I won, I took the kid to school, and if Hastings won, he took the fifty and the kid."

Marion flushed quickly. She realized that Tex Blanco had risked fifty dollars for a chance to bring little Jimmy to school — to meet her.

"Why did you do that?" she asked.

"Well, I didn't want to be sorry, yuh know. And I think at lot of Jimmy, don't I, Jimmy?"

"Yes, Uncle Tex," said Jimmy gravely.

"Shake hands with Miss Evans, Jimmy."

The little boy shook hands solemnly with her.

"Pleased to meetcha," he said.

"And I'm pleased to meet you, Jimmy."

" 'At's good. Uncle Tex says I've gotta learn a lot, so I won't have to be no cowpuncher all my life."

"Oh, I'm sure you will learn very fast, Jimmy."

“ ’At’s good.”

“Well, here comes the board of trustees,” laughed Tex. “I’ll leave Jimmy to you, Miss Evans — and gladly.”

He swung his horse around, waved a gloved hand at Jimmy, and rode away from town. Marion stood there with Jimmy, waiting for the three trustees, and again the children began their noise inside the school house. Marion realized that they were quiet while Tex Blanco had been there.

The three men came up to the porch, and she knew they had been discussing the reasons for Tex Blanco being there.

“Good mornin’,” greeted Hootie. “How’s everythin’ comin’?”

“Oh, just fine. This little boy is from Mr. Blanco’s ranch. His name is Jimmy Hastings.”

“Oh, that’s why Tex was here, eh? We wondered.”

“Yuh hadn’t ought to have much to do with him, ma’am,” advised Henry Goff, the postmaster.

“Them things,” pronounced Hootie coldly, “is personal matters, Hennery. We hired this lady to teach school, yuh must remember.”

“I know, but —”

“Drop it, Henry,” advised Sam Hall. “Any old time you start preachin’ morals, I’ll tell about the time you slickeared a branded calf.”

“Never did! By golly, I — I —”

“Yore loop’s dragging’,” cautioned Hootie. “We never came up here to recite our pasts to Miss Evans, but to have her prove a problem. Here it is, Miss Evans:

There's a room with eight corners, and in each corner sets a cat. Each cat looks at seven cats. How many cats in the room?"

Marion laughed outright. "Why, eight, of course."

"Eight?" wondered Henry. "But there's eight to start with."

"Of course. And each one looks at the other seven."

"Seventy-two!" exploded Sam Hall. "Seventy-two!"

"You didn't know, you animated jew's harp!" snapped Henry.

"I admit it," laughed Sam. "But I knowed it wasn't seventy-two."

"Well, we better go back and let the lady start her school," said Hootie. "It's a cinch she knows more than we do."

"About cats," amended Sam Hall.

"Come any time," said Marion, laughing.

"Any time Sam Hall gets a problem," laughed Hootie.

Marion spent the entire day in trying to get the grades separated and to get some semblance of order in the place. There was no chance for study, and her mind was in a whirl, when the day was over, and the children went whooping outdoors, all except little Jimmy, who stayed in his seat.

"Aren't you going out too, Jimmy?" she asked.

"Gotta wait for Uncle Tex."

"Oh, is he coming after you, Jimmy?"

"He won me for a month."

"Won you for a month?"

"That's what he said," solemnly. "And he squeezed me so hard he almost busted a rib. Did anybody ever squeeze you that hard?"

"I'm afraid not, Jimmy," laughing.

"Uncle Tex is awful strong. I like to ride with him."

"You seem to like your Uncle Tex, Jimmy."

"'At's right. He told me he was takin' me to learn somethin' from a beautiful lady. I guess he meant you."

"But I'm not beautiful, Jimmy."

"Well," Jimmy frowned thoughtfully. He was trying to remember something he had heard one of the cowboys say about a girl.

"Well, you ain't hard to look at."

"Where in the world did you ever heard such a thing? Did your Uncle Tex say that?"

"N'm. I guess it was Kit Carson. He's pretty tough."

"And who is Kit Carson, Jimmy?"

"Oh, he's one of Uncle Tex's saddle-slickers."

A noise at the front of the building caused Marion to look up, and she saw Tex Blanco stepping up to the door. He was wearing that flame-colored shirt again, and the sun sparkled on his silver-trimmed chaps. He stopped in the doorway and smiled widely, as he doffed his wide hat.

"I came to get my winnings," he said to Marion, and came inside. "Was he a good boy, ma'am?"

"Just lovely," smiled Marion.

Jimmy slid out of his seat and stood beside Tex. His tousled head just reached the bottom of Tex's holster, from which peeped the butt of a pearl-handled revolver, which flashed like fire-opal in a beam of sunlight through a window pane.

"I understand you have won him for a month," said Marion seriously.

Tex looked steadily at her for several moments, before he looked down at Jimmy.

"Yea-a-h," he said slowly. "Jimmy tol yuh, ma'am?"

"Well, you did," declared Jimmy. "You told me, Uncle Tex."

"That's right, old pardner; I did tell yuh."

Tex looked up at Marion. "You don't mind, do yuh, ma'am?"

"If you bring Jimmy to school?"

"Yeah."

"That is your business, Mr. Blanco."

"I'm awful glad to meet somebody who concedes me some rights, ma'am. You'll hear lots of things about me. After yuh hear all of it, mebby yuh won't concede me the right to bring Jimmy to school."

"I have already heard many things," she said slowly. "Still I don't understand why you should gamble for the chance to bring the little boy to school."

"Don'tcha, ma'am? Well" — Tex took a deep breath and patted Jimmy on the head fondly — "you prob'ly learned a lot from books. A lady must be pretty smart to teach school — but there's some things that you don't know yet. C'mon, Jimmy."

They turned and walked straight through the doorway, and Marion saw Tex toss Jimmy to the saddle, before climbing on. She bowed her head on her arms and tried to laugh, but the laugh did not come. It was ridiculous for Tex Blanco, the killer, to come to the school twice a day, merely to see her. She knew what the people would say. She didn't want to see him. He was nothing to her — never would be.

She arranged her desk and put on her hat, but she sat there quite a while, her eyes fixed on the spot beside little Jimmy's desk, where the sunlight glinted through a window, like a spotlight trained on the floor. She could still visualize Tex Blanco's white-tooth smile above the flame-color of his shirt, and the sunlight flashing back from the pearl handle of his big revolver.

Finally she got to her feet and walked out, locking the door behind her. It was nearly a quarter of a mile walk to Hootie Cooper's house, but she did not hurry. Cleve Tolman and two of his men rode past her on the gallop, almost blinding her in a cloud of dust.

"They might at least have slowed down," she told herself angrily. "I'll bet Tex Blanco wouldn't have done it."

And then she grew angry with herself for thinking of Tex Blanco. She was still flushed when she reached home, where she found Mrs. Cooper on the wide porch, fanning herself with a huge straw hat.

"I been wonderin' how yuh was gettin' along, Marion," said Mrs. Cooper. "Sit down and tell me all about it."

Marion was only too glad to sink down in one of their easy chairs and remove her hat.

"Well, I suppose everything went as it usually does on the opening day of school, Ma Cooper. It is quite a task to get them all placed."

"I'll betcha. I'd use a barrel stave, m'self."

Mrs. Cooper fanned herself industriously for a moment.

"Hootie was tellin' me that Tex Blanco brought the little Hastings boy to school."

"And came after him a while ago," said Marion.

"Yea-a-ah?" Mrs. Cooper turned her head and looked at Marion closely. "Came and got him, eh? Is Andy Hastings crippled, or somethin'?"

"Tex Blanco gambled with little Jimmy's father, and Tex Blanco won the right to bring Jimmy to school for one whole month."

"For one whole month?" Mrs. Cooper's face slowly dissolved into a smile; the smile into a chuckling laugh.

"Mamma mine!" she chuckled. "Oh, can yuh beat that? For one whole month. That's shore a new one. Gambled for a chance to see you twice a day."

"But I don't want to see him," declared Marion.

Mrs. Cooper looked closely at Marion.

"Of course yuh don't, dearie. I'll speak to Hootie about it tonight. He'll see that Tex don't bother yuh. Hootie likes Tex, and all that, but he'll jist explain it to Tex in a nice way, and I'll bet he quits annoyin' yuh."

"But he — he wasn't annoying me. It is just the fact that he — that he comes to the school, you see."

"I see. Well, we can stop that. Just you quit worryin' about Tex Blanco. I don't think he ever had a girl before."

"But I'm *not* his girl, don't you see?"

"That's right. You've probably got a feller in the east."

"No, I haven't."

"Well," smiled Mrs. Cooper, "we'll have Hootie tell Tex that yuh have."

"But that would be lying."

"Huh? Oh, yeah — lyin'."

Mrs. Cooper smiled broadly and shook her head. "Yo're funny. I try to get yuh out of bein' embarrassed, and yuh won't let me. Just between me and you, we've got to stop Tex from comin' to see yuh — even at the school. Folks might talk, don'tcha see? You don't realize that Tex is sort of an outcast around here — a man with a bad reputation. You can't afford to have yore name linked with his, can yuh?"

"Certainly not."

"I should say yuh couldn't," sighed Mrs. Cooper. "But ain't he good lookin', Marion. He's the kind of a man I used to dream about — and look what I got. Dreams shore go by contraries. Hootie's got a heart as big as an ox, and I reckon the rest of his internal organs are in the right place, but as a specimen he shore don't stack up beside Tex Blanco. I love Hootie, but my love ain't blind."

Marion laughed softly. "Looks are not everything."

"Well, they're quite a lot, Marion. Your looks made Tex Blanco gamble for the chance to see yuh."

"From what I hear, that is not much to brag about."

"Well, I'm glad yo're level-headed. Some girls might fall for his looks. You'll meet the right man some day. Can't teach school all yore life. Probably get one with bow legs and a mole on his nose. Cleve Tolman asked me quite a lot about you. He's interested. Asked me about yore family, but I didn't know anythin' to tell him. Tex didn't ask. He's the kind that would take yuh, even if yuh never had any folks."

Marion flushed and grew interested in a broken stitch on her glove.

"There isn't much to tell about my family," she said slowly. "Father died a few months after I was born, and I guess mother had a hard time making a living for my brother and me. He was older than me. We got along somehow, back there in Chicago. We all worked, and I went to night school after my brother left home and my mother died."

"Well, you had a hard time, didn't yuh? Mother and father both dead, eh?"

"Yes — both gone."

"Where's yore brother?"

"Who knows? He left home when I was fourteen."

"And never told yuh where he went?"

"No. You see, he — he had to leave. Oh, we're not so good," she said bitterly. "He was suspected of a robbery. The police came for him, but he got away. It killed mother. She just sort of faded away after that, and a year later she died. I was fifteen then and getting five dollars a week in a department store.

"But I managed to live, and I went to night school, until I got my diploma. I kept on working, saving what little I could. I knew I could never qualify as a teacher in a big city; so I came to Cheyenne: I don't know why I ever selected Cheyenne. There I learned about Pineville and their need of a teacher for this term of school. Oh, it was a godsend to me. I just had one silver dollar when I arrived."

Marion was on the verge of tears when she finished her story.

"I didn't intend to tell any one my story," she said; "but I just had to tell you, Ma Cooper."

"Well, I'm glad yuh did, Honey. It seems as though I've known you all yore life. Yore face was familiar the first time I ever seen yuh. Now, you go in and clean up, while I start mixin' a flock of biscuits. Hootie likes 'em, and if I do say it myself, I mingle a good one. Mebby we better let things go as they lie for a while — about Tex Blanco."

"Perhaps it would be best, Ma Cooper. I don't want to hurt his feelings."

"Shore, yuh don't. Some folks say he hasn't any, but they're crazy."

"Little Jimmy Hastings certainly loves him."

"And I've seen dogs follerin' him. You run along, Honey."

Marion kissed Mrs. Cooper and went into the house. The fat lady dropped the straw hat in a chair, took a deep breath and grinned widely at nothing at all. Then she went in and began' mixing biscuits.

CHAPTER FIVE

It was several days later that five men sat in the sheriff's office, with the front door closed. There were Pat Lynch, the sheriff, Mort Heffner, prosecuting attorney, Cleve Tolman, Shorty Gallup and a detective named Sears, from the cattle association.

Sears was a slender man, about forty years of age, rather grim of visage. He had arrived that day from Cheyenne, and wanted a few details. Tolman and Gallup happened to be in from the TD ranch; so the sheriff asked them to talk with Sears.

"How did yuh happen to get a detective?" asked Tolman, after Sears had been introduced.

"I sent for him," replied Heffner. "We talked it over, the Sheriff and myself. As far as I could see, we were not getting anywhere in the solving of Buck Dennig's murder; so we decided to appeal to the association. Of course, the county will pay part of the expenses. We thought a range detective would be better than one from a private bureau."

"And I'm going to need help," smiled Sears. "Coming in on a case so late in the day, when all evidence is stale, I am going to need a lot of information. The sheriff has outlined things to me, of course; but only the bare facts. Mr. Dennig was your partner, was he not?"

"Yeah, he was my pardner," said Tolman.

"You understand his financial condition, I take it."

"What do you mean?"

"As I understand it, Mr. Dennig drew ten thousand dollars from the bank on the afternoon of his murder."

"He did," said Tolman shortly.

"Have you any idea why he drew all this money?"

"No idea at all. Didn't know he drew it, until after the murder."

"I believe he had the sum of one hundred and sixty dollars on his body. Doesn't it seem that some one knew he had this money, and robbed him?"

"You'd naturally think so."

"Was he in the habit of carrying a big sum on his person?"

"I don't think he was."

"Was this partnership money, or his own?"

"His own. We didn't have any partnership account."

"I see. You don't know that he owed any such a sum?"

Tolman smiled shortly. "Not that I knew anythin' about."

"Do you know how much money he had left in the bank after drawing this sum?"

"About five thousand, I understand."

"Mr. Tolman, do you think Dennig was killed for his money, or for revenge?"

"How would I know?"

"I understand Mr. Dennig had no relatives; no one to leave his share of the ranch. Is that true?"

"That's true."

"And you naturally receive his share."

"Well?"

"Have you done anything personally to try and find out who killed him, Mr. Tolman?"

"That's the law's business, Mr. Sears — not mine."

"And yet you profit greatly, do you not?"

Tolman got to his feet quickly, facing the detective.

"That's about all of that," he said harshly. "It's no fault of mine that Buck Dennig had no relatives. Was it my fault that he had no will? You talk as though I had somethin' to do with his murder. You can go to hell with the rest of yore questions. C'mon, Shorty."

Tolman kicked the door open and strode out, followed by Shorty, who was grinning foolishly. Sears watched them across the street to the Stormy River saloon.

"You got under his hide," grinned the sheriff. "Now you'll get no more information from Cleve Tolman."

"Didn't get anything worth while, anyway, Sheriff."

"You don't think he had anything to do with it, do you?" asked Heffner.

"Well, he got mad, didn't he? You were in that poker game when Dennig and Blanco quarrelled. Weren't you, Heffner?"

"Yes, I was there."

"Dennig accused Blanco of stealing, didn't he?"

"He did. They were both mad, and I really believe there would have been a killing right there if we hadn't interfered."

"And it was only an hour or so after that, I understand, that Dennig started home. He didn't exhibit a lot of money in the saloon that night, did he?"

"Not over a couple of hundred dollars. He came to town early in the afternoon. Buck wasn't a heavy drinker, but this time he had quite a few. No, he wasn't drunk, but he just had enough to make him rather savage. He certainly called Tex Blanco a lot of fighting names that night."

"Did Blanco have much to say back to him?"

"Not so much. Tex isn't foul-mouthed, you know. But he was mad. I don't blame him. The things Buck Dennig called him would make a jack-rabbit bite a grizzly bear."

"Blanco has rather a sinister reputation, I understand."

"I suppose he has."

"And there has been hard feelings between the TD and the Blanco outfits for quite a while, I understand."

"The TD claim they lost cattle," said the sheriff. "They never came right out and accused Blanco, of course, and they never asked my help in the matter."

Sears nodded thoughtfully. "Don't seem to be much to work on in this case, but I'll do what I can."

But Sears met with little success in his investigations. Always the suspicion pointed at Tex Blanco, but there was no evidence. Sears did not go out to see Tex. He rode out to the TD ranch, but learned nothing. In fact, Tolman gave him to understand that a detective was not welcome on the TD.

He had been in Pineville three days, when a letter was sent to him in care of the sheriff. It had been posted in Pineville, and read: —

"We will give you eight hours to leave this valley.
"THE BUNCH."

"I guess that settles it," said Sears nervously.

"Looks thataway," agreed the sheriff grimly, studying the pencilled note.

He sent Oscar after Heffner, who came immediately, and they discussed the note seriously.

"What would you do, Heffner?" asked Sears.

"I'd leave here," said Heffner. "I guess you've found that you can't do us any good, and there's no use of getting killed, Sears. The Bunch mean business, I guess. The stage leaves for Garnet at one o'clock; so you better slide out gracefully."

And Sears slid. He went to the Pineville Hotel to pack his bags, leaving the note with Heffner, who put it in his pocket.

They walked up to the bank and called Shearer aside.

"Have you a copy of Tex Blanco's signature, Shearer?" asked Heffner.

"Certainly."

"Let us look at it, please."

Shearer produced the card with Blanco's signature, and went to wait on a customer, while Heffner compared it with the writing on the pencilled note.

"Look at that B," whispered Heffner. A comparison of the B in "Bunch" and the B in "Blanco" showed them to be nearly alike.

They gave the card back to Shearer and went back to the office.

"Goin' to show it to Sears?" asked the sheriff.

"No, I don't think I will. We've got to move slow in this, Pat. It would require a handwriting expert to prove that Tex Blanco made that B — and then you'd have a hard job proving it to a cow jury. No, we've got to have more than that, but it sure gives us plenty of reasons for keeping an eye on Tex Blanco."

"Well, he's in town twice a day," smiled the sheriff. "He brings Andy Hastings' little boy to school every morning and comes after him at four o'clock."

"What's the idea, Pat?"

"The new teacher."

"Miss Evans? You don't mean to say he's stuck on her?"

"Nothin' strange about that, is there? My God, if I was twenty years younger I'd find some kid to take to school."

"But Tex Blanco — that's different," laughed Heffner. "Somebody ought to talk to the lady about it."

"Suppose you try it, Mort."

"Not me. I'm happily married — and somebody might think I was jealous."

That afternoon Sears left Pineville, riding on the seat with Windy March, having accomplished nothing. He believed implicitly in warnings, and had no hankering for a bullet in his back. They met Tex Blanco between town and the B Arrow ranch, and Sears felt a contraction of the spine, until a curve in the road hid them from view.

"Do you think Tex Blanco killed Dennig?" he asked Windy.

"Well, I'll tell yuh," said Windy seriously. "The road is most always dusty this time of year. We need rain."

"That seems to be the general opinion," replied Sears, and added quickly: "That we need rain."

Windy spat over the wheel and cleared his throat. "You through detectin'?"

"I'm leavin' the valley."

"I didn't think yuh would stay long. I allus had an idea that a detective was kinda sneakin'."

"You mean, he didn't let anybody know who he was?"

"Yeah — wore whiskers and looks for nicks on the furniture."

Sears laughed. "Well, I suppose that is one way to do it. I was warned to get out inside of eight hours."

"Yea-a-ah? Well, well! Warned, eh? When didja get this here warnin'?"

"About eleven o'clock this morning."

"Well," Windy squinted at the sun, "I'll say yuh gave yourself plenty of leeway, pardner."

It did not require many days for every one in Pineville to know that Tex Blanco was coming to the school twice a day, and the gossips had plenty of material. Marion heard none of the talk. She was too busy these days. But Ma Cooper heard it. Hootie heard it too, and was worried. He talked it over with his wife.

"They're talkin' too much," declared Hootie. "It'll hurt Marion; hurt the school. Puts me in an awful hole, Ma. Sam and Henry both talked with me today about it."

"I'll speak to Marion, Hootie. She ain't to blame. Darn the whole bunch of old forked tongues around here, anyway!"

But Marion did not need to be told. That morning, after she had called the roll, she discovered that Joe and Mary Beebee were not present. She asked little Ella Hall, who lived next door to Beebee, if she knew why they were absent.

"Their ma took them out, Miss Evans," piped the little girl. "She told my ma this morning that she wasn't never going to let them come to this school any more."

"My gracious — and why not, Ella?"

"She said it was because Tex Blanco came here. She said to my ma —"

"That will do, Ella. Thank you so much."

Marion looked blankly down at the litter of papers on her desk, her mind in a whirl.

"My ma said —" began little Ella, but Marion stopped her.

"That will be all, Ella. We — we will dispense with the singing this morning."

"What did she say about my Uncle Tex?" piped little Jimmy Hastings.

"Nothing, Jimmy. Go right ahead with your studies."

"'At's good."

Jimmy glared at the back of Ella's head, but finally subsided behind a book, held tightly in his chubby hands.

That day was interminably long to Marion. She did not go home to lunch. At recess and noon the children talked in whispers, with Ella Hall the centre of their conversation.

Marion dismissed school fifteen minutes early. She wanted time to plan what to say to Tex Blanco. She did not know he was there, until she happened to lift her eyes and saw him standing in the doorway. Jimmy was drawing a picture on his slate, and the only sound was the creak and scratch of his slate pencil.

"Hallo," said Tex softly. Jimmy turned his head and looked at him.

"C'mere, Uncle Tex," he piped. "See what I drawed of Ella Hall."

Tex came slowly up to him, looking at the slate.

"Yuh shore gave her plenty mouth, pardner," said Tex.

"She's mouthy," declared Jimmy.

Tex looked at Marion and laughed. But Marion was not laughing. Tex sobered quickly and walked toward her.

"What's the matter?" he asked.

"You must not come here any more," she said wearily.

"Not come here, ma'am?"

"Not any more, Mr. Blanco."

"I don't understand what yuh mean."

"Old lady Beebee took her two kids out of school 'cause you come here," said Jimmy. "I heard Ella Hall tell all the kids outdoors. She said you was stuck on Miss Evans, and that you wasn't fit for much, and that she wouldn't let her kids come to school. By golly, I shore told her somethin'. Ella said her pa was a trustee and she'd have me throwed out. Can she, Miss Evans?"

For several minutes Tex and Marion looked at each other. The eyes of the big cowboy were clouded, his lips tightly shut. He turned from Marion and stared at the blackboard.

"Oh, I'm sorry," he said hoarsely. "I didn't know. I was a fool to do this. I might have known all the time. I'm just a — not fit. With the reputation I've got, I should never have looked at you. But, Gawd A'mighty, I'm human.

"No matter what they say about me, I'm just human. The happiest week of my life has been in bringin' little pardner down here to school — and seein' you twice a day. But I didn't know it would turn out like this. I used to sing, a long time ago — I've been singin' for a week now. Mother said she'd like to meet you — to meet the girl who brought back her singin' cowboy.

"But that's all past now. I'm sorry I hurt yuh, ma'am. I won't come any more. You can tell 'em that for me. Jimmy's pa will bring him in the mornin'. Good-bye."

He took little Jimmy by the hand and they walked out, without a backward glance; the tall cowboy in the flame-colored shirt, his fine shoulders dropped just a little, and the little boy, his head tilted as he looked up at his big partner.

"I shore told Ella Hall where to head in at, Uncle Tex," she heard him say.

"Thank you, little pardner."

And then they rode away; the little boy who did not quite understand, and the singing cowboy, who had lost his song.

Marion leaned forward on her desk, chin in her hands, her eyes filled with tears.

"Oh, why don't people mind their own business?" she asked herself. "Why don't they? But they never have — not since time began; so what can you expect?"

She did not say anything to Ma Cooper about it that night; not even after she heard that the trustees were to have a meeting at Sam Hall's house.

It was a rare occasion when Hootie Cooper took a drink, but this night he came home partly saturated. From her room Marion heard some of the conversation between Hootie and Ma Cooper.

"I ain't drunk, Ma," she heard him tell her. "But I came within about three swallers of it. I offered to lick old Sam and Hennery, with one hand tied behind me. Darn 'em! Old lady Beebee was there. Yea-a-ah, shore! I told 'em what I thought of the whole danged works, resigned as a trustee, and drank straight whiskey to celebrate m' return from bondage."

"But what did they decide to do, Hootie?"

"They've appointed old man Beebee to fill my place, and they're goin' to plant the seats of their pants on the school house steps in the mornin', and when Tex shows up they're goin' to tell him what for."

"Ain't you goin' to undress before yuh go to bed, Hootie?"

"Oh, yeah. Ma, if they say anythin' to hurt Marion, I'll whip hell out of the whole works."

"You couldn't whip anythin'."

"I might s'prise yuh."

"Yuh shore would. If I was you, I'd unbutton that shirt before I tried to take it off."

"The darn thing has shrunk, Ma."

"No such a thing. You take them suspenders off yore shoulders, and it'll come off all right."

The following morning the three trustees were there. They did not come in the school house, but sat on the edge of the porch. Old man Beebee — possibly fifty, but looking seventy — with a thin crop of whiskers, bald head, sour face; Sam Hall, nasal voiced, red-tipped nose; Henry Goff, querulous, argumentative; three old buzzards waiting for the kill.

And they waited too; waited until five minutes of nine, while the blacksmith shop remained unopened, and folks wondered why the post office was still closed.

Then came Andy Hastings and Jimmy. He put Jimmy on the school-house steps and rode away, as the bell rung and the children trooped in.

"Reckon I better git to the shop," drawled Sam Hall.

"Same here," said Henry. "Folks'll wonder where I am."

"Somebody," said Beebee seriously, "must have told Tex Blanco."

"Probably was Hootie Cooper," growled Henry. "That man ain't got a damn bit of civic pride."

They went tramping back along the dusty road, while Marion watched them from the window, a half-smile on her face. Little Jimmy sat very straight in his seat, his eyes on the Beebee children and Ella Hall, who stuck out her tongue at the teacher's back.

Crash! Marion whirled in time to see a pencil box rebound off the top of Ella's desk, scattering pencils in every direction. Jimmy was on his feet, his eyes snapping.

"Who threw that box?" asked Marion.

"Jimmy Hastings," said Joe Beebee. "I seen him, teacher."

"Yo're dern right I throwed it," piped Jimmy bravely. "And it didn't hit where I meant fer it to either."

"He threw it right at me," declared Joe.

"Yo're a lyin' chuckwalla!" shrilled Jimmy. "I throwed it at Ella Hall. She stuck her tongue at the teacher."

Marion struck the side of a seat with a ruler.

"Be quiet, all of you!"

She came slowly over to Jimmy and looked down at him.

"Why did you do that, Jimmy?"

He looked up at her, his blue eyes very brave and earnest.

"I don't let nobody run a blazer on you," he said.

Marion walked away and sat down at her desk. There was no punishment meted out that time. Joe Beebe stayed around the school house that night until Andy

Hastings took Jimmy home, and Marion knew he had been instructed to wait and see if Tex Blanco came after the little boy.

That night Mrs. Cooper asked Marion to ride to Garnet with her on Saturday.

"I want to see if I can get somethin' different for a new dress," she told Marion. "Hootie won't keep no stock. Says that everybody sends to a mail-order house for their stuff, anyway. We can get an early start from here and git back early in the afternoon."

Marion was glad to go. Hootie heard about the trustees waiting until nine o'clock for Tex, and gurgled with joy. It was his idea of a good joke. Of course, he did not know why Tex didn't come.

"I had a invite for yuh, Marion," he told her. "Cleve Tolman asked me if I thought you'd go to Garnet with him to a dance tomorrow night."

"I don't reckon Marion wants any second-hand invitations," said Ma Cooper quickly.

"Not any, thanks," laughed Marion.

"I can tell him that?"

"Certainly."

"Well," laughed Ma Cooper, "I had the same thing put to me by Oscar Johnson, and I told him he better ask yuh himself. They're all scared of yuh, Marion."

"And Lester Cline wants to meet yuh," grinned Hootie. "I told him he'd wait a long time for me to introduce him. He's my rival in everythin', except kerosene. Some day he'll burn out like I did, and then he'll quit handlin' it."

CHAPTER SIX

The next two days were uneventful. Things were going smoothly at the school. Marion saw nothing of Tex Blanco, but she did see Cleve Tolman, and from his cold nod, she concluded that Hootie had told him her decision regarding the dance invitation.

Came Saturday morning, and the ride to Garnet. Mrs. Cooper was a capable driver, and Hootie's buckskin team, hitched to a buckboard, desired nothing so much as open road and plenty of it. Mrs. Cooper weighted down one side of the seat so badly that Marion felt herself perched high on the opposite side, where she clung to the seat with one hand, her hat with the other.

They made the trip to Garnet in record time, and spent the rest of the forenoon in shopping at Garnet's two small stores, and watching one train go through. They ate at a Chinese restaurant, where they met Windy March. He had been at the dance the night before, and was red-eyed.

"Shore had a good time," he told them. "You should have been there, Miss Evans."

"Why didn't yuh ask her to go?" queried Ma Cooper.

"Why — uh — by golly, I didn't think she'd go. I heard she turned down Cleve Tolman."

"News," pronounced Ma Cooper, "shore does get around. Was Cleve Tolman there, Windy?"

"Nope. Annie Hall came with Lester Cline. Oscar Johnson came alone, and hated Lester all evenin'. Annie won't go with Oscar, since he tried to kill her in Pat Lynch's buckboard. She's kinda walked with a hitch ever since."

"Treat 'em rough, that's Oscar," laughed Ma Cooper.

Windy finished his lunch and went out to his stage duties. He drove out of town about fifteen minutes ahead of them, going back to Pineville.

"We'll let him get well ahead," said Ma Cooper. "That road ain't wide enough to do much passin' on, and we don't want to eat his dirt all the way home."

The buckskins were still willing to travel, and they knew they were going home. Mile after mile they reeled off at a steady trot, fighting against the pull of the bits, until they came to a stiff pull up a winding grade, where they slowed to a walk.

Once over the top they surged into a trot again across the mesa. At the far side of the mesa, where the road wound down to the valley level again, Ma Cooper drew up the team for a breathing spell.

Below them the yellow ribbon of road wound in and out through the clumps of brush, and far beyond, marked by a patch of green, was the B Arrow ranch. Farther along was the green ribbon, which marked the course of Stormy River.

"Why, there is the stage down there!" exclaimed Marion, pointing down the hill. "See it down there, just beyond that little ravine."

"I see it," said Ma Cooper. Their's was almost a bird's-eye view of the stage, which was not over three hundred yards from them, on an air-line. It appeared as though the driver was sitting very straight on the seat, with both hands in the air.

For several moments they watched the scene below them. Then Ma Cooper fairly exploded: —

"A hold up! Can't yuh see it, Marion? My Lord! There's a man just back of the stage. Can yuh see him?"

"Yes, I can see him," nervously.

They saw the driver's arms drop down, and the stage lurched ahead, the driver still sitting stiffly, apparently looking straight ahead.

"But where is the man who was behind the stage?" wondered Marion.

"He hit for the brush. I'll betcha they saw us."

For possibly ten minutes they sat and watched the brushy country below them, but caught no sight of the man. Far out toward the B Arrow Ranch trailed the dust cloud of the fast travelling stage.

"Well, that's that," declared Ma Cooper. "That's the first hold up I ever seen. Giddap-broncs."

"But aren't you afraid to pass that spot?" asked Marion.

"Good grief — no! They've pulled out a long time ago."

They stopped where the tracks of the stage had turned slightly off the road.

"This is the place where they stopped," said Ma Cooper.

But Marion did not express an opinion. Her eyes were riveted on something just beyond the fresh tire marks of the stage, where the sunlight flashed back the colors of a fire opal.

Slowly she dismounted from the buckboard and went over to it.

"What is it, Marion?" asked Ma Cooper. Marion came back with the heavy Colt revolver in her hand.

"Either Windy or the robber dropped it!" exclaimed Ma Cooper. "And it don't look like a gun Windy March might own. Golly, ain't them handles pretty Say, what's the matter with yuh, Marion? Too much sun?"

Marion tried to speak, but finally shook her head, as she rested one hand against the wheel of the buckboard.

"What in the world is the matter with yuh, Honey?"

"Didn't you ever see that gun?" asked Marion weakly.

"Not to my knowledge. Did you?"

"It — it's Tex Blanco's gun."

"Whooee-ee! Tex Blanco's gun? Then Tex —"

Ma Cooper did not finish. She leaned across the seat and touched Marion on the arm.

"Get in here," she said. Marion obeyed, holding the gun in both hands.

"I didn't know how yuh felt, Honey," said Ma Cooper. "That evidence would send Tex up for several years. This here is *our* secret. We'll throw that gun in the river, and forget it."

Marion nodded dumbly. "You are awfully good, Ma Cooper."

"You forget that part of it. I'm not so damn good — I'm jist human, Honey. Just remember that we never seen no hold up. Are yuh sure about that gun?"

"I think so, Ma. He — he carried one just like it."

"Any man is a fool to pack a gun yuh can identify him by, anyway. And that's a gaudy thing. I never had any jewellery half as gaudy as them handles. Giddap, broncs."

And while Ma Cooper and Marion Evans drove on to Pineville, Windy March galloped his four horses down the main street of town and drew up at the post office. Windy had experienced his first hold up, and he wanted everybody in the town to hear about it.

Luckily the sheriff and deputy were at the office, and came on the run, when some one yelled through their doorway that the stage had been robbed. Inside of three minutes the stage was surrounded, listening to Windy tell how it happened.

"Jist at the bottom, this side of the mesa," he told them. "Rope tied across the road belly-high to a bronc, and with a cloth danglin' from it. My leaders comes to a stop. And then I hears a voice from the brush, a'tellin' me to put up my hands and keep lookin' ahead. They also tells me that if I look around I'll see Saint Peter.

"Not bein' wishful to see him, I does as I'm told. I'm sure there's two men, 'cause I hears 'em whisperin'. They shore took everythin' they wanted. My little, old strong box is gone, I know that much. Then they told me to look east and keep lookin' east, or I'd git a quick chance to visit some of my very, very old ancestors. After a while I hears one of 'em say: —

" 'All right; look up the road again.' And then I seen that the rope was gone.

" 'Drive straight ahead and don't look back,' said one of 'em, and that's what I done. I tell yuh, they knowed what they was doin'. I never seen a danged one of 'em, and their voices sounded like they had a bad cold."

"At this side of the mesa, eh?" queried the sheriff.

"Jist at the bottom, Sheriff. I reckon you can see where I swung a little off the road."

The sheriff and deputy ran to the stable, saddled their horses, equipped themselves with rifles, and headed out of town. The sheriff knew there was little use of trying to do anything, but it seemed that the public expected them to at least make a show of doing something.

Just at the Stormy River ford they met Ma Cooper and Marion, and waited for the buckboard to make the crossing. Ma Cooper drew up the team.

"Did you jist come from Garnets," asked the sheriff.

"We shore did," laughed Ma Cooper. "All the way."

"How far were you behind the stage, Mrs. Cooper?"

"I dunno. Windy drove away about fifteen minutes ahead of us. Why?"

"He was held up at this side of the mesa. You was lucky not to run into it?"

"Good grief! Held up, yuh say? What did they get?"

"I didn't stop to find out. We're just ridin' foolish, I suppose."

They lifted their hats and rode on across the river, while Ma Cooper chuckled to herself.

"Well, I didn't have to lie, did I, Honey? They didn't ask me if we saw it. And if we hadn't seen them first, they might have seen you dump that gun in the river — if you had tried to dump it. Now, what'll we do with it?"

"I shall keep it," said Marion. "Down in the bottom of my trunk, Ma. It's as safe there as it would be in the river."

"That's fine. Wrap it up in a piece of paper and get it in the trunk as fast as you can. Half the people in this country prob'ly know Tex Blanco packs that kind of a gun, and if the sheriff knew yuh had it, he'd put two and two together and figure yuh found it at the hold up."

"I could swear that Tex Blanco gave it to me."

"Don't be silly! Even in this country, men don't make girls presents of forty-five Colts. Keep it hid."

"Oh, I suppose I'm foolish," said Marion. "It doesn't make him any less the criminal."

"You'd be surprised to know how many honest men are criminals, Honey. And a man ain't a criminal until he's caught. Go ahead and be foolish. That's a woman's privilege, when a certain man is concerned."

But the sheriff found nothing, except where the stage had turned out — and a woman's tracks in the sand. There were men's tracks too, but they meant nothing in the dust and sand. The woman had a small foot and wore high-heels.

The marks of the buckboard, with its narrow tires, also cut the outside of the road, and the tracks led from these.

"What do yuh make of them?" asked Oscar, the deputy.

The sheriff shook his head thoughtfully. "I dunno. Them two wimmin stopped here in the buckboard, and one of them walked over there. The tracks show she walked straight out there and straight back. She either found somethin', or she walked out there to look at somethin'."

"Mebby we better ask 'em, Pat."

"Mm-m-m. You don't know much about wimmin, do yuh, Oscar? If yuh did, you'd know better. Either their answer wouldn't be worth a damn to us, or they wouldn't tell."

"That ain't Mrs. Cooper's feet prints," said Oscar. "She wears a flat-heel shoe."

"You ort to be a detective, Oscar."

"Yeah, I reckon so. I could do as well as Sears did. Do yuh reckon this hold up was pulled by the bunch who sent the note to Sears?"

"I hope so, Oscar. I'd hate to think that there was two tough outfits in our little country. Now, lemme see. They'd likely pull south-west from here; so we'll take a little ride down thataway and see what we can pick up."

But after an hour or so of fruitless riding, they swung in past the B Arrow Ranch, where they found Andy Hastings putting a new brace on the big ranch house gate. He was working alone; so they stopped to talk with him.

After a few minutes of general conversation, the sheriff asked him if Tex was at home.

"I ain't seen him today," said Andy. "He went to the dance at Garnet last night, I think. Prob'ly got into a poker game and stayed all night. What's new, Pat?"

"Nothin' much, Andy. How's the little kid gettin' along in school?"

"Jimmy? He's doin' fine. Tells me he's had sev-ral good fights already, and thinks education is a great thing for a man. He's shore strong for the new teacher. Wants to give her a horse; so she can go ridin' with him."

"Lotsa punchers around here feel the same about it," grinned Oscar. "She could have a swell remuda, if she'd jist do a little acceptin'. I'd start it with a couple good broncs, myself."

"I'll betcha," grinned Andy.

"Here comes Tex now," said the sheriff, as a horse and rider came into view down the road.

Tex was riding slowly, and as he drew closer they could see that his face was rather pale. His gray sombrero was drawn rather rakishly over one eye, and he did not smile. It was rather unusual for Tex not to smile. He merely nodded shortly to them and rode through the gate. They watched him dismount stiffly at the stable and lead his horse inside.

"Must 'a' had a hard night," smiled the sheriff.

"I sh'd say he has!" exclaimed Andy. "It ain't like old Tex to act thataway. Hm-m-m. Well, it's his business."

"Shore is," nodded Oscar. "See yuh later, Andy."

"Yeah. Drop in any time."

They rode on toward Pineville, and when they were out of earshot of the ranch, Oscar turned to the sheriff.

"What do yuh think of that?"

"Think of what, Oscar?"

"Tex has been in a mix up, Pat. Didn't yuh notice how he was wearin' his hat? Coverin' a bump, I'll betcha. And his neckerchief had blood spots on it too. And not only that, but he didn't have no gun in his holster."

"I didn't notice," confessed the sheriff.

"And he looked as though he had slept in his clothes."

"Oscar," seriously, "you ought to be a detective."

"Well, mebby that's true — but I ain't."

"Do yuh think we ought to go back and ask Tex what happened to him?"

"Not now, Paddy. With that expression on his face, I'd be scared to even ask him what time it is. That's the first time I ever seen Tex without his smile."

"That's true. Keep still about them tracks in the sand, Oscar. And don't say anythin' about Tex. If we're ever goin' to put the deadwood on anybody, we've got to stop tellin' the world what we suspect."

"Well, I'm jist a-tellin' yuh; so yuh *would* know."

Luke Jones straightened up and kicked the oven door shut with a bang. Standing in the kitchen doorway was Shorty Gallup, a limp cigarette hanging in the corner of his mouth.

"Yuh think so, do yuh?" he sneered.

"I don't think nothin' about it — I know! You may be foreman of this damn TD Ranch, but I'm foreman of this kitchen. Don't come around here a-tellin' me what to do, or how to do it. By God, I was cookin' food for he-men, when you wasn't weaned yet."

"Oh, you can cook — if yuh want to, Luke. But yo're layin' down on the job. Cleve knows it. We was talkin' about it last night."

"The hell yuh was! You and Cleve, eh? Lissen t' me, Shorty; any old time I don't suit Cleve Tolman, he can come and tell me; and not send a dirty-eared puncher to pack his messages. Yes, yuh are. You ain't washed further back than the front of yore face since yuh owned yore first pair of chaps. You jist run along and be foreman of the cows."

Shorty snorted disgustedly and went down to the corral, where Eddie Grimes and Matt Sturgis were fooling around with a hammer-headed buckskin. Shorty sauntered into the corral and leaned against the fence.

"Whatcha goin' to do with him?" he asked.

"Goin' to ride him," grunted Matt, working up the rope.

"Eddie goin' to ride him?"

There was a sneer in Shorty's question. Eddie did not pretend to be a bronc rider.

"I'm goin' to ride him," said Matt.

"I thought so."

Shorty came over, took hold of the rope and shoved Eddie aside.

"You better go and set on the fence," he said roughly, and then added maliciously: "And let the men do the work."

Matt laughed. Eddie let loose of the rope, but made no move to get away.

"Git to hell out of here!" snapped Shorty. "Ain't yuh even got sense enough to take an order?"

"Not that kind of an order," replied Eddie evenly.

Matt turned and looked at Eddie, whose back was partly turned to him, and winked at Shorty.

"What kind of an order do yuh need?" queried Shorty.

"White man's talk, Shorty. You talk like a baby."

Shorty had gathered up the slack of the lariat, and now he slashed Eddie across the face. It was a cowardly thing to do, but did little damage, except to blind Eddie for a moment, and in that moment Shorty dropped the rope and sprang in, trying to hit Eddie with his fists.

Eddie backed away, blocking the blows with his elbows, bobbing his head up and down to escape the flying fists, but quickly got set and came back, swapping punches with Shorty.

Neither of them showed any science. It was just a case of slug, slug, slug, with both men trying to send over a finishing blow. And it was Eddie who landed it. One of his wild uppercuts crashed against the point of Shorty's jaw, and the TD foreman went to his haunches.

And almost at the same moment Matt Sturgis smashed Eddie between the angle of his jaw and the ear, and Eddie went down on his hands and knees, too, dazed to realize that Shorty had surged to his feet and was trying to kick him.

"That's kinda dirty, don'tcha think?" asked a voice.

Shorty turned quickly, blinking his still dazed eyes at the two cowboys who had ridden up close to the fence, and were looking at him with great disapproval. Eddie got to his feet, wondering what it was all about.

The men were strangers to the cowboys in the corral, but Shorty was still so dazed and angry that he blurted: —

"Don't horn in on somethin' that's none of yore business."

"I suppose not," said the taller of the two riders easily, "but just the same it shore looked like a dirty trick to me, pardner."

"Well, I'll be danged!" Shorty came over closer to the fence and stared at the strangers.

The one who had done all the talking was well over six feet tall, rather slender, with a long, serious face, level gray eyes and a wide mouth. The other was shorter, broad of shoulder, with a rather blocky face, creased heavily with grin-wrinkles, his blue eyes rather large and inquiring.

The tall one rode a tall gray horse, the short one a sorrel, and behind them was a bay mare, carrying a pack. Both men were dressed in range clothes, and both needed a shave.

Eddie Grimes walked over to the gate and let himself out of the corral, while Shorty and Matt considered the strangers.

"Jist about where in hell did you come from?" demanded Shorty.

"That," said the tall, grayed-eyed one, "is our business; if yo're so particular about personal business."

"Is that so?" Shorty felt of his damaged jaw tenderly. Matt Sturgis had nothing to say, but shifted uneasily from one foot to the other under the steady stare of the gray eyes.

"Is that the road to Pineville out there?"

Matt nodded quickly. The tall cowboy gave Shorty a sharp glance, before he turned his horse and rode away from the corral. Eddie Grimes was coming from the bunk-house, carrying his war sack in one hand. He called to the strangers: —

"Are you goin' to Pineville?"

"Shore am," replied the tall cowboy.

"Wait a minute and I'll ride with yuh, if yuh don't mind; I'm through with this place."

"Yo're darn right yuh are!" yelled Shorty.

Eddie looked toward the corral, laughed shortly and looked at the strangers.

"He's the foreman of this ranch."

They waited until Eddie had saddled his horse, while Shorty and Matt watched them from between the poles of the corral. Eddie rode up to the kitchen door and called to old Luke, who came to the doorway.

"I'm pullin' out, Luke," he said.

"Yeah? Well, be good to yourself, Eddie. I don't blame yuh."

"I'll probably see yuh soon again, Luke."

"Shore. I may not stay long m'self. *Adios*."

Eddie rode toward the gate and the strangers followed him out.

"This is the TD Ranch," explained Eddie as he fastened the gate behind them. "The foreman's name is Gallup — Shorty Gallup. That other pole-cat is named Matt Sturgis. My name is Eddie Grimes."

He swung back on his horse and the tall cowboy shook hands with him.

"My name's Hartley," he said. "My pardner is Stevens.

Eddie shook hands with him, and they headed for Pineville.

"I'm glad you showed up when yuh did," grinned Eddie. "Yuh see, I wasn't lookin' for Matt to pop me thataway."

"And Mr. Gallup was aimin' to put the boots to yuh, I observed."

"I guess he was."

"We came across the range from Piney Lake," said Hartley. "Never been over here before. We struck that creek this side of the summit and follered it all the way to the ranch."

"Lobo Creek," said Eddie. "Quite a trip over from Piney Lake."

"Took us two days. How are things over there, Grimes?"

"All right, I guess. I've been with the TD for quite a while. Everythin' was fine until Buck Dennig got killed, and Cleve Tolman hired Shorty Gallup as a foreman."

"Not much good, eh?"

"Overbearin' little devil. He got whipped a short time ago by Frank Judd, of the B Arrow. Thinks he's a fighter, and is always lookin' for trouble. I'll have to come back and get my wages from Tolman, I suppose."

"How did this Dennig get killed?"

"Murdered. Somebody smashed him on the head one night and stole ten thousand dollars from him. Nobody knows who done it."

"Hashknife, we must be in a land of milk and honey," laughed Stevens. "Cowboys packing ten thousand!"

"Well, it ain't a common thing," laughed Eddie.

"Don't mind Sleepy," grinned Hashknife Hartley. "He's always jumpin' at conclusions."

"Buck was the first man I ever knew who carried that much money," said Eddie.

"Wasn't anythin' done to find out who killed him?" asked Hashknife curiously.

"Sure. The sheriff talked with the prosecutin' attorney, and they both talked with Cleve Tolman. They held an inquest and decided that Buck had been murdered. Then the cattle association sent a detective over here, and he lasted long enough to be warned out of the valley."

Hashknife laughed softly. "You've had quite a lot of excitement around here, it seems."

"Plenty. Day before yesterday the stage was held up between Garnet and Pineville and three thousand taken. The sheriff rode down, looked over the spot where the robbery had taken place, and came home."

"A very unmoral place," sighed Hashknife.

"You ain't a preacher, are yuh?" asked Eddie quickly.

Hashknife laughed and shook his head. "Not by any means, Grimes. My father was a minister. He rode the Milk River Range, packin' the Gospel and a Winchester. Sort of a bunk-house sky-pilot, yuh know. Me, I'm just a puncher, thasall."

"Lookin' for work?"

"Bein' kinda lazy — no. We might take a job."

"There's a vacancy at the TD, yuh know."

"Yeah, I know; but I am afraid the foreman might not want my services. Anyway, there's two of us."

"That's right. I'm afraid you'll have a hard job gettin' on here for the winter."

"Mebby we won't want to," said Sleepy Stevens. "I shore don't want to spend no winter in a place where they hold up folks. I scare easy."

Eddie Grimes looked sideways at the broad shoulders and the square jaw of Sleepy Stevens; noting the heavy Colt in its weathered holster, the easy sway of the body, which is only acquired by years in the saddle.

"I'll bet you do," agreed Eddie.

"Any old time they start trouble, I've shore got a lot of goin' away to do," said Sleepy seriously.

Just before they reached Pineville they met Cleve Tolman, riding alone. He looked curiously at Hashknife and Sleepy, but Grimes did not introduce him.

"I quit the TD a little while ago," he told Tolman.

"Quit, eh? Kinda sudden, wasn't it, Eddie?"

"I suppose yuh might say it was, Cleve. Had a run-in with Shorty. Him and Matt kinda double-teamed on me."

"Yea-a-ah?" Tolman looked him over curiously. "You don't seem to be hurt much."

"No, I didn't get hurt much, Cleve."

"Shorty fire yuh?"

"I quit. And I don't mind tellin' yuh that you'll lose more men, unless you fire Shorty."

"I'll run my own business," said Tolman shortly. He looked straight at Hashknife, but Grimes did not offer to introduce them. Tolman reached in his pocket and drew out a wallet.

"I owe you about thirty-five dollars," he said, and gave the money to Grimes.

"You better tell Shorty to lay off Luke, or you'll lose yore cook," said Grimes, pocketing the money.

"I can run my own business, Grimes."

"Mebby yuh can, Cleve."

"No mebby about it."

Tolman nodded shortly and rode on.

"That's the man who inherited Buck Dennig's half of the TD," said Grimes, as they rode on toward town.

Hashknife looked curiously at Grimes, but did not ask him just why he said that. It sounded as though Tolman might have had something to do with Buck's demise.

"Wasn't anybody hurt in the stage robbery, was there?" asked Hashknife.

Grimes laughed shortly. "No shots fired. Windy March was scared half to death, I reckon. Got something to talk about for the rest of his life, though."

CHAPTER SEVEN

They rode to Pineville, where Hashknife and Sleepy stabled their horses and secured a room at the Pineville Hotel. The sheriff had seen them ride in, and he was just a little curious about who they were; so he appeared at the hotel, where Grimes had also secured a room, and Grimes was accommodating enough to introduce them.

"I saw yuh come in," said the sheriff. "Prospectin'?"

"No-o-o," said Hashknife thoughtfully. "Yuh see, we ain't got no shovel."

"I noticed yuh didn't," seriously.

"We rode in over the divide from Piney Lake," said Hashknife. "Follered down Lobo Creek and hit the TD."

"Aimin' for Pineville, eh?"

"Well, not exactly; just aimin' to hit this valley."

"Never been here before?"

"Never have, sheriff. Nice little town you've got here."

" 'Sall right, Hartley. Goin' to be here a while?"

"Couple days, prob'ly. We're just lookin' around."

"Fine. Make my office yore headquarters while yo're in town, will yuh?"

"Thanks."

The sheriff went away, and they headed for a restaurant.

"It strikes me that yore sheriff is full of questions," grinned Hashknife.

"Oh, shore," laughed Grimes. "Pat's a question box. But he's all right. You'll like him fine. He's got a big Swede deputy, and they quarrel about all the time. Both good men, but they don't think very fast.

"Pat is kinda touchy about the killin' of Dennig and this stage robbery. He don't know which way to turn; so he stands still. Mebby that's the best thing to do, after all."

They ate their meal and wandered around the town. The stage came in, and with the driver was an angular sort of a person, with a black mustache and a large nose. Hashknife, Sleepy and Grimes walked past the stage, while Windy was taking off the mail, and spoke to the black moustached passenger.

"Hello, Alex. How's everythin' in Wallgate?"

"All right, Eddie. How's everythin' at the ranch?"

"Same as ever. I quit today."

"The hell yuh did! What's the matter?"

"Too much foreman."

The man laughed, as he climbed down from the stage.

"I don't blame yuh," he said seriously.

"How's yore brother, Alex?"

"Gittin' along fine, Eddie — thanks."

They strolled along and Grimes told them that this was Alex McLean, one of the TD cowboys, whose brother had been very sick at Wallgate, twenty miles south of Garnet, and McLean had been down to see him.

"Alex is a good man," declared Grimes. "About the first time Shorty tries to ride him, he'll bust Shorty wide open."

McLean watched the three men walk down the street, and turned to the post office, where he met the sheriff.

"Hello, Alex," grinned the sheriff. "How's yore brother?"

"Gettin' along fine, Pat. Wasn't as bad as they thought he was. Kinda hard to kill a Scot. Do yuh know who them two strange cowboys are with Eddie Grimes?"

"Oh, I met 'em a while ago, Alex. Hartley and Stevens. They came in from Piney Lake. Came over the divide and follered Lobo Creek to the TD."

"Yea-a-ah?" Alex shifted his black brows slightly, shut one eye and appeared to be thinking deeply.

"Piney Lake, eh? They told you that, Pat?"

"Sure."

"Hm-m-m. Piney Lake, eh? By golly, they shore cut one big circle. I seen 'em in Wallgate three days ago."

"In Wallgate three days — yuh shore about that, Alex?"

"They ain't a pair to mistake very easy, Pat."

"Three days ago, eh? And they rode in from Piney Lake. If they left Wallgate three days ago, they couldn't have got to Piney Lake short of two days, even if they went over Lobo Pass — and that's the way they came back."

"That's right, Pat."

"Mm-m-m-m. Alex, do me a favor, will yuh? Don't say nothin' about this to anybody? You heard about the stage bein' stuck up for three thousand dollars, didn't yuh?"

"I did."

"Well, don't say anythin'."

"That's an order with me, Pat. I'm headin' for the ranch right away, and if yuh want me — I'm there; sabe?"

"Thank yuh, Alex."

But Alex was not very reliable. He had a number of drinks at the Stormy River saloon and took a quart of liquor with him, when he went to the livery stable after his horse. Several of the boys were at the TD when he arrived, and they all went to the bunk-house with Alex, who was just drunk enough to be talkative.

"I seen Eddie in town," he told Shorty, who felt of his tender jaw and took a deep drink.

"Said he quit."

"I fired him," declared Shorty. "Wasn't worth a damn. He ain't got no nerve."

"Throwed in with a couple strangers," said Alex.

"Thasso?" Shorty did not mention the fact that he had seen the two strangers.

"Did you bring that bottle specially for Shorty?" asked Bud Severn.

"Take it," growled Shorty, passing it to Bud, who took a drink and passed the bottle to Matt Sturgis.

"Who were the strangers?" asked Bud.

"I dunno," grinned Alex. "Couple awful damn liars, Bud. Said they come over the hill from Piney Lake. That's a two-day trip."

"Yo're drunk," grunted Bud. "Or did they tell yuh they made it in a day?"

"They didn't tell me nothin'; but they told the sheriff they come over the hump from Piney Lake."

"Better cache that bottle," advised Bud.

"Think I'm drunk, do yuh?" grinned Alex. "Well, listen t' me, will yuh? I seen them two jiggers in Wallgate three days ago. If they came here from Piney Lake, they shore flewed. My gee-og-ri-fee may not be the best there is in the world, but —"

"They couldn't do it," declared Shorty.

"That's what the sheriff thinks."

"Ain't none of his business if a man wants to lie," said Bud. "Gimme back that bottle, Matt."

"Mebbe he'll make it his business," grinned Alex. "Yuh must remember that two men held up the stage two days ago, and it's only twenty mile from Wallgate to Garnet."

"Well, that's different," grunted Bud, wiping off the neck of the bottle on his sleeve.

"But why in hell would they come back here for?" queried Alex. "That beats me."

"Mebby they thought there was more easy money in this valley," said Shorty. "That's my opinion, but I never told nobody outside of my own gang."

"Yo're a lot like the feller who said he had confided his secret to only one party — the Republican party," laughed Bud.

"Well, I know it won't go no further," said Alex, trying to get the cork in the empty bottle.

"You better lay down and sleep it off," advised Shorty.

In the meantime the sheriff was undecided what to do. Hashknife and Sleepy came down to his office and made themselves at home, talking intelligently about his office and its duties; so much so, in fact, that he was just a little suspicious that they were pumping him.

They did not mention any of the things which had been worrying him, and finally went away, promising to come again. He went to Heffner's office and laid the facts, as he had them from McLean, before the prosecuting attorney, who sucked on the butt of a cheap cigar, his feet on the desk top.

"No evidence there," decided Heffner. "Man has a perfect right to lie, Pat. At least that seems to be the general opinion in a cow country. Do they look like suspicious characters?"

"No, they don't, Mort. The tall one looks plumb through yuh, and the other one laughs at yuh. But it strikes me that if they wanted to rob a stage, all hell wouldn't stop that stage from bein' robbed. I saw the brands on their horses, and looked 'em up in the registry; but they ain't from this state. They're goin' to be here a few days, so they told me."

"Well, just keep an eye on 'em, Pat. If they start gambling, watch their money. That three thousand was mostly in twenty dollar gold certificates."

"I'll watch out for that. Have you been doin' any thinkin' about Buck Dennig's money, Mort. Somebody around here has that money; and the man who has it is the man who killed poor old Buck. But I can't think of anythin' to do."

Heffner shook his head slowly. "Not an idea, Pat. I wish we had a detective. I don't mean one like Sears."

"He wouldn't stand a chance — no more than Sears did."

"Not if he was known. Sears was a fool to tell who he was."

"What else could he do? He was a stranger here."

"That's true, Pat. I suppose we'll have to go along in our dumb way, leaving it unsolved."

But Pat didn't agree with him. Heffner was too much inclined to let things slip along. The sheriff had very little detective ability, usually thinking in a single-track way, but he had known and admired Buck Dennig for a long time, and he wanted to convict the man who had murdered him. And he had also done considerable speculating over those tracks he had found beside the road, where the stage had been robbed. For some reason he thought that Marion Evans and Mrs. Cooper knew something.

Hashknife and Sleepy wandered around and finally entered Hootie Cooper's store, where they purchased some tobacco. Hashknife eyed Hootie closely. He had noted the name on the store sign, and now he said: —

"You don't happen to be any relation to Jim Cooper, who runs a store in Mizpa, Arizona, do yuh?"

"Hootie's eyes opened wide and his face broke into a wide smile.

"Jim Cooper of Mizpa is my brother. You know him?"

"Bought tobacco from him all last winter," laughed Hashknife. "My name's Hartley, Mr. Cooper."

They shook hands warmly, and Sleepy was introduced.

"I thought you two looked alike," said Hashknife.

"Well, I'll be darned!" exploded Hootie. "And you know old Jim, eh? Older 'n me. Ain't seen him for five year. How was he?"

"Fine, the last time we seen him."

"Well, gosh! Say! I'm shore glad to meetcha. Didja just arrive here?"

"Today."

"Stayin' at the hotel?"

"Goin' to," smiled Hashknife.

"Good. Yo're both comin' over to my house and have supper with us tonight. I'll tell Ma right away. No, yuh can't lie out of it. We've got to talk. I shut up this shebang at six o'clock, and you meet me here. Nobody there, except Ma and the school ma'am. Mighty nice girl too. She's folks."

"Well, that's shore nice of yuh," smiled Hashknife.

"Shucks! Ma'll be glad to see yuh. She likes Jim. She was jist sayin' the other day that I ought to write a letter to Jim; but he's owed me one for four year. We ain't much on letter writin'. You meet me here at six, or I'll shore comb this town for yuh."

They promised to meet him at that time, and went to the hotel to shave and clean up a little.

"Gotta look smooth to greet the school ma'am," laughed Sleepy.

"Yeah, and you'll prob'ly fall in love with her," grinned Hashknife, emptying his war bag in search of a clean shirt. "You mostly always do, Sleepy."

"Not with school ma'ams, cowboy. There's where I draw the line."

Sleepy began industriously stropping at his razor, whistling unmusically.

"How do yuh like the looks of this place, Sleepy?" asked Hashknife.

"Cow-town and no trimmin's. Some nice folks. Say! I was just wonderin' about this Jim Cooper of Mizpa. I don't remember him, Hashknife."

"You remember Mizpa, don'tcha?"

"Well, we was there that one day, Hashknife."

"Sure. Remember the wind storm that day?"

"Yea-a-ah. Say, I forgot that. Wasn't it a dinger? That was the time the sign blowed off the store and almost landed on us, wasn't it?"

"That's the time."

"But I don't remember no Jim Cooper."

"His name was on that sign."

Sleepy chuckled softly and began lathering his face.

"You shore got a memory, Hashknife," he said.

"Well," grinned Hashknife, "I seen them two words, painted in big letters 'Jim Cooper' sailin' right straight for my head; so I ought to remember him. Mebby we didn't meet Jim Cooper, but we shore met a sign-board by that name."

"And now you've got to talk all evenin' about Jim Cooper."

"Not necessarily; we can change the subject. You can get in a corner and talk to the teacher."

"Any time I do! I may be a lady's man, but I'm no teacher's pet. You can have her."

"Is that a promise?" laughed Hashknife.

"Yeah — and a gift, cowboy."

They met Hootie at the store at six o'clock and went home with him. He had told Mrs. Cooper about them, and she welcomed them pleasantly.

"Small world, ain't it?" she laughed. "Funny how you just happened to mention Jim to Hootie. Lotsa Coopers, yuh know."

"Yeah, I know it," smiled Hashknife. "But Jim Cooper had the biggest sign I ever seen. Letters two feet high."

"He would have," chuckled Hootie. "Prob'ly spent a lot of time across the street, lookin' at that sign."

"Gents, I want you to meet Miss Evans," said Mrs. Cooper. "Miss Evans is the school teacher. Mr. Hartley and Mr. Stevens."

"Oh, I am pleased to meet both of you," said Marion.

"So'm I," said Sleepy foolishly. Hashknife caught his eye and said softly: —

"And a gift, Sleepy — remember."

Marion excused herself to help Mrs. Cooper, and Sleepy whistled softly.

"Mamma mine, what a looker!"

"Ain't she nice?" said Hootie softly. "Jist as nice as she looks too."

"How do yuh keep the cowboys away?" asked Hashknife.

"They're scared of her — she's too pretty, Hartley."

"Mm-m-m-m. That's a new way of gettin' rid of 'em."

"Oh, they're shyin' around. Do yuh know" — Hootie dropped his voice and moved in closer — "wimmin' are queer. She could prob'ly pick any man in this valley, and I'll be danged if I don't think she's stuck on Tex Blanco."

"Not knowin' Tex Blanco, I don't sabe yore remark," smiled Hashknife.

"Oh, that's right." Hootie rubbed his nose thoughtfully. "I dunno how I come to mention it to you, anyway; bein' as yo're a stranger. Anyway, this Tex Blanco is supposed to be a pretty bad hombre. Lotsa folks think he killed Dennig. I don't know a thing about it, but he ain't thought much of around here. Owns the B Arrow Ranch, yuh know."

"Beauty and the beast, eh?" smiled Hashknife.

"Well, I dunno about that. But ain't it funny that she would pick *him?*"

"It probably isn't a bit funny to her."

"No, that's right."

Mrs. Cooper called them in to eat supper, and seated Sleepy beside Marion. It ruined Sleepy's meal. The talk was general, but Sleepy said nothing. Hootie talked with Hashknife about Jim Cooper, and Hashknife bravely kept up his end of the conversation, even if he didn't know Jim. Ma Cooper believed in the stuffing process, and both cowboys did their best to please her.

Marion helped Ma Cooper clear away the dishes, leaving the three men at the table enjoying a smoke. Sleepy's face was still damp with perspiration, and he felt like a man who had just been dragged from a watery grave. The women had gone into the living room, while the three men were in a deep discussion, and they heard a man's voice.

The discussion stopped quickly. Hootie listened for a moment.

"The sheriff," he said softly, but made no effort to get up from the table. The sheriff was saying: —

"I thought I'd just drop in for a minute, Mrs. Cooper. There's somethin' that's been botherin' me. It's about that stage robbery the other day. You was the only folks over the road jist after the robbery, yuh know.

"Well, me and Oscar went right out there. Yuh remember we met yuh at the ford. Well, we found where the stage had been robbed, and we found where you had swung off the road a little in yore buckboard. And one of yuh, I reckon it was Miss Evans, got out of the buckboard, walked about ten feet off to one side, and then came back to the buckboard. Anyway, I reckon it was Miss Evans, because she's the only woman in this country that wears them sharp-pointed high heels. Now, Miss Evans; jist what did you find out there?"

The three men strained their ears for her answer.

"I — I don't know what you mean," she faltered.

"Certainly not!" snapped Ma Cooper. "Of all things! You got a lot of nerve, Pat Lynch."

"I just wanted an answer," said the sheriff mildly.

"Nope."

"Well, you've got it, ain't yuh?"

Marion started to say something, but Ma Cooper stopped her.

"You let me talk to him."

"Well, you tell it, Mrs. Cooper," said the sheriff.

"There's nothin' to tell. Yo're crazy."

"Mebby. But the tracks are there. Mebby yuh forgot about tracks."

"Mebby," said Mrs. Cooper shortly.

"All I'm tryin' to do is to find out what Miss Evans picked up. The tracks show —"

"Since when did you start bein' a trailer?" asked Mrs. Cooper. "Readin' tracks — the idea!"

"Oh, I could read 'em plain enough."

Hootie got to his feet, and the two cowboys followed him through the doorway. The sheriff was standing beside the door, and he reddened slightly at sight of the three men.

"You ain't tryin' to pin somethin' on the wimmin', are yuh, Pat?" grinned Hootie.

The sheriff shifted his feet nervously.

"I just came to ask a question, Hootie."

"I heard yuh say that before, Pat. Well, you got yore answer, didn't yuh?"

"I got a kind of an answer."

"That's all anybody ever gets from a woman."

"I reckon so," sighed the sheriff. He twisted his hat in his hands for a moment, before looking at Ma Cooper.

"I wish you'd think it over, Mrs. Cooper," he said. "Yuh know there's a law against destroyin' evidence. Compoundin' a felony, they call it. Think it over, will yuh? Good-night."

He opened the door and stepped outside, closing the door behind him. Hashknife was watching Marion closely, and he knew she was frightened. She looked appealingly at Mrs. Cooper, caught Hashknife's steady gaze and turned her head away.

"What's it all about, Ma?" asked Hootie.

"You heard what he said, didn't yuh? That's all I know. C'mon, Marion. Gee, he sure settled my supper. I thought we was goin' to be arrested."

Marion followed her into the kitchen, and they shut the door between that and the dining room. Hootie filled his pipe thoughtfully, frowning to himself. Finally he grinned at Hashknife and shook his head.

"Wimmin' are funny, Hartley."

"I suppose they are — most of 'em."

"That sheriff had his nerve — accusin' women," declared Sleepy warmly.

"Well, he won't get anythin' out of Ma," chuckled Hootie. "That woman can *keep* a secret."

"Do yuh think she's got one to keep?" smiled Hashknife.

"If she ain't, I don't know her. Any time Ma gets mad and talks real fast — she's coverin' up somethin'. But it ain't nothin' bad. Nossir. Compoundin' a felony!

Mebby he thinks Ma and Marion held up the stage. Tonight I'm going to ask Ma for my split of the three thousand, or I'll squeal on both of 'em."

Hootie laughed and dropped his pipe on the carpet.

"Set down, boys. I dunno what we're all standin' up here for, when there's plenty of chairs. I'll bet Pat Lynch forgot that I told him you was goin' to eat supper with us. I told him you was a old friend of my brother Jim, down in Mizpa, Arizona. He don't know Jim."

"Pretty good sheriff, ain't he?"

"Fills the office. Never caught nobody that I ever heard about. But we ain't had much crime. Yeah, I reckon Pat is as good as the average."

Ma Cooper and Marion stayed in the kitchen long enough to regain their composure before coming back to the living room, but it was easy to see that Marion was disturbed.

"Did yuh ever hear a more ridiculous thing?" asked Ma Cooper. "The nerve of Pat Lynch! Why, he acted as though *we* held up the old stage."

She turned to Hashknife. "I don't know what you boys will think of us," she said.

"I think yo're mighty good cooks," smiled Hashknife. "As far as the sheriff is concerned, let's forget him."

"Aw, he wouldn't know a woman's track from a buggy track, said Sleepy. "Hoppin' on a woman thataway! And even if yuh did make tracks in his old sand, and if yuh picked up somethin', and if yuh did — did —"

"Now, yo're all tied up in a string," laughed Hashknife. "He means well, folks."

"Well, you know what I mean," said Sleepy lamely.

They stayed about an hour after supper, and went back to their hotel.

"Ain't she a dinger?" asked Sleepy, sprawling on the bed. "Mamma mine, ain't she a peach, Hashknife?"

Hashknife slumped down in a chair, his shoulders even with his ears, as he puffed on a cigarette, his eyes half-closed.

"What do yuh suppose she picked up, Hashknife?"

But Hashknife did not reply to Sleepy's question. And Sleepy would have been greatly surprised if he had, because Hashknife was not strong for suppositions.

"Jist my luck," mused Sleepy, staring at the ceiling. "Here I am, a honest, industrious, clean-minded cowboy, with a big heart and a soul filled with lovin' kindness, comin' in jist too late. Mopped out of a chance of matrimony by a danged outlaw. Virtue is its *own* reward, I suppose."

"Then you think she picked this Tex Blanco, because it was sort of a last resort, do yuh?" asked Hashknife.

"I never thought about that. Are you goin' to bed?"

"I sure am, Sleepy. I can hear them blankets callin' to me right now."

"Yeah; and you hear somethin' else callin' to yuh."

Hashknife smiled softly, as he drew off his high-heel boots.

"We're a queer pair of birdies, Sleepy," he said. "Always goin' some place, and never gettin' there."

"And we pray to the God of the trails untrod," quoted Sleepy.

"That's it, cowboy; the trails untrod; the other side of the hill. I'm gettin' gray hairs, and I like to set down and talk about the old bunch. That's a sign of age, they tell me."

"Shore is." Tugging at a refractory boot. "Old age! By God, that's somethin' I hate to look forward to. We can't afford to grow old, Hashknife. You must have been forty yore last birthday."

"Forty-one. And you'll be forty pretty soon. The span of a man's life is three score years and ten, they say."

"A peaceable life," grunted Sleepy. "Not our kind."

"A peaceable life. Must be great to just drift along from one day to the next, puttin' up money for old age; no dangers, nobody shootin' at yuh — just peace every day."

"Suppose we try it — some day."

"Some day — sure. Get in; I'll blow out the lamp."

They had been together a long time, these two. Drifting up and down the open lands of the West from the Alberta ranges to the Mexican border; always on the move; never content to stay long in any place.

Hashknife was originally from the Milk River country in Montana, while Sleepy was from Idaho. Fate drew David Stevens to the Hashknife ranch, where he met Henry Hartley, who was nicknamed after that brand, and together they started out to see what was on the other side of the hill.

Because of the fact that he seemed always awake, Dave was nicknamed Sleepy. They were intensely human, these two, and their sense of humor had carried them over many hard bumps. They had gambled with Fate and had won so many times that they were confirmed fatalists.

Hashknife was the leader. Born with a keen mind, he had developed it through observation, studying human nature, especially human failings, to a point where the mere mention of a mystery would cause him to abandon any other plans he might have to solve it.

But Hashknife was not a man hunter. He had no interest in reward notices, no extreme dislike for a criminal. To him it was just the things that happen in the world; the pendulum of Fate, which makes both saint and sinner in the same mould.

Together they would solve a mystery — and ride on. They asked no reward. Sometimes they would work for a cattle outfit for a while, gathering in a few dollars before riding on. Their partnership had not been remunerative. In fact, they were poorer in pocket than they were the day they rode away together. But they did not care. They realized that they were pawns of Fate, moving hither and thither around the board, doing their little bit to help to make the world better.

"We've never been in a place where they wouldn't welcome us back, Sleepy," said Hashknife. "Mebby, when we're old, we'll swing back, goin' over the hill from the other direction."

CHAPTER EIGHT

The following day was a trial for Marion. It was one of those days when every one in the school seemed to be on edge. Two of the larger boys started a fight in the yard, and she sent them both home with notes to their parents. Marion did not feel physically able to whip them, as they were nearly as big as she.

And to cap the climax, at noon came Mrs. Beebee and Mrs. Hall, wives of the trustees. Mrs. Hall was as large as Mrs. Cooper; a great, grim-faced woman, dressed in black, with a small hat, which she had trimmed herself; a weird and wonderful creation of artificial wheat, red cherries and a single ostrich plume; the whole balanced precariously on the back of her head.

Mrs. Beebee was a thin, scrawny little woman, dressed in rusty black, with a parrot-like voice and a hooked nose, which increased the illusion of her vocal cords. They nodded grimly to Marion and sat down at a vacant seat at the rear of the room.

"Visitin'," said Mrs. Beebee severely.

"Oh, I am glad you came," said Marion, trying to be pleasant.

"Mm-m-m-m," said Mrs. Hall dryly and dubiously.

And there they sat all the afternoon, saying nothing, listening closely to everything. The children seemed to sense the strain too; and went bad accordingly. Marion had always had trouble with Joe and Mary Beebee, but today they seemed doubly possessed of demons.

Everything went wrong. No one had their lessons. Even Ella Hall, the school tattle-tale, who was usually letter perfect, failed utterly, and tried to prove an alibi by openly telling the teacher she had given her too much work.

And Marion was too miserable to reprimand her; so Ella went back to her seat, her tongue in her cheek, while the black-clad judges in the rear seat looked at each other understandingly. After three hours of this, Marion was ready to scream.

She dismissed school at the regular time, expecting that her visitors would stay long enough to at least express an opinion, but they trailed out with the children and she watched them from the window, going stiffly down the street, bobbing their heads, as they talked it over, while Ella, Joe and Mary stayed close to them, apparently getting an earful of what was being said.

Marion sighed and looked down at little Jimmy Hastings, who was waiting for his father. Jimmy's face seemed flushed and he rested his chin on his folded arms.

"Don't you feel well, Jimmy?" she asked.

"Not very, ma'am. My head kinda aches. And I'm mad too." He sat up in his seat, fumbling with his books.

"You must never get mad, Jimmy," she said.

" 'At's all right. I heard 'em talkin' at recess. Mary Beebee said she'd bet that it won't be long before we have a new teacher. She said her ma and Mrs. Hall came up here to see if you was doin' yore work right."

Marion's heart sank just a little. She realized that these two women would be able to influence their husbands enough to cause them to make a change. She had no contract with the Pineville School Board. And if they did, she would not even have money enough to take her back to Cheyenne.

"And Ella Hall said her mother wasn't satisfied with what you'd done to Ella," said Jimmy slowly. "Gee, I don't want you to go away."

"Well, I don't want to go away, Jimmy. But I think it will all turn out right."

"Mebby. Uncle Tex thinks you're a dinger. Sometimes he talks with me about yuh. He says I'm learnin' awful fast. You ain't seen him for quite a while, have yuh? He ain't been to town. Somebody" — Jimmy's eyes grew wide and round — "hit him on the head, don'tcha know it."

"Somebody hit him on the head, Jimmy?"

"Yes'm. Had a big lump on the side of his head. He never told nobody how he got it. I heard Frank Judd and Tommy Corbett talkin' about it. It was the day the stage was held up. I asked him what happened, but he wouldn't tell me."

"I didn't know anything about it," said Marion.

"And he ain't got that pretty gun no more," said Jimmy. "Gee, 'at was a pretty gun."

"And Tex liked it an awful lot," said Jimmy, after a few moments of reflection. "He likes pretty things."

"Is your Uncle Tex a good singer, Jimmy?"

"Y'betcha — when he feels like it. He used to sing to me, when he was bringing' me to school. Most always it was somethin' about Mother Mac — somethin'."

"Mother Machree, Jimmy?"

"That's her. He said it was the Irish croppin' out. What did he mean by that, Miss Evans?"

"Isn't he part Irish, Jimmy?"

"I dunno." Jimmy yawned widely.

"Here comes your father," said Marion, glancing through the window.

Jimmy met him at the doorway, and they went away together on the horse. Marion closed the school-house and went home. She found Ma Cooper on the porch, dressed in a voluminous wrapper, reading a cook book. Marion sat down on the steps and took off her hat.

"Yuh had company today, didn't yuh?" asked Ma.

Marion sighed deeply and placed her hat on the steps.

"Yes," she said sadly. "Mrs. Beebee and Mrs. Hall."

"Came to pick yuh to pieces, eh?"

"Oh, I suppose. And there were plenty of opportunities. The children were possessed today, Ma."

"They would be — with those two there. I took one look at the two old buzzards and said to myself that you was in for a pleasant afternoon, unless I missed my guess. Some day I'm goin' to tell 'em both what I think of 'em. Poor old Beebee. He'll have about as much chance to be a trustee as I will. Same with old Sam

Hall. It'll be Mrs. Beebee and Mrs. Hall against old Henry Goff — and he won't count. I'm glad Hootie's off the board. Old Henry ought to git off too. He ain't got no kids."

"If Mrs. Beebee and Mrs. Hall decided to — to make a change in teachers, could they let me go?" asked Marion.

"Well, I wouldn't think of such a thing, Marion. It's been a hard job to get any teacher in Pineville. Don't you worry about it for a minute."

"I don't know. There is a lot of talk among the pupils, instigated, of course, by Mary and Joe Beebee and Ella Hall. Where there is so much smoke, there must be a little fire. And I can't afford to lose this position, Ma Cooper."

"Oh, you won't lose it. Quit worryin'. Change yore clothes and come back here where it's cool."

That evening Hashknife saw Tex Blanco for the first time. Tex had ridden in with Frank Judd and Tommy Corbett, who had met with Eddie Grimes and Sleepy, while Hashknife had been visiting with the sheriff.

Tex was in a restaurant, eating his supper, when Hashknife and the sheriff came in. He spoke pleasantly to the sheriff, gave Hashknife a sharp glance and continued eating. Hashknife was rather impressed with Tex's appearance. There was nothing of the ignorant, gun-man type about Tex.

They sat down at the rear of the room and ordered their supper. Hashknife had a feeling that the sheriff had been trying to find out more about him, and he wondered just why the sheriff would be curious about him. He had asked Hashknife about the places he and Sleepy had worked, and his eyes expressed disbelief, when Hashknife began enumerating more brands than the average cowboy ever dreamed of seeing.

"You must have kept movin' pretty reg'lar," said the sheriff dryly.

"Did."

"What was the idea of movin' so often, Hartley?"

"The hill that was just ahead."

"The hill that was — I don't get what yuh mean."

"We wanted to see the other side."

"Oh, yeah. Kinda tramps, eh?"

"Mebby. I don't just like that word."

"Mebby not. How long are yuh goin' to stay here?"

"*Quien sabe?* Mebby pretty soon we'll see a hill ahead."

Tex left the restaurant, and in a few minutes Shorty Gallup, Bud Severn and Alex McLean came in. They had been drinking and were in a boisterous mood.

"Hyah, sheriff!" yelled Shorty. When he opened his mouth it showed two teeth missing in front.

"Hallo, Shorty," said the sheriff. Shorty looked at Hashknife closely, said something to Alex McLean, and they all sat down at a table near the front of the room.

The sheriff was a little nervous, and hurried through his supper. He didn't like the idea of the TD and the B Arrow gangs meeting in Pineville. After they left the restaurant the sheriff confided this to Hashknife.

"Oscar is in Garnet," he told Hashknife. "Ought to be back pretty soon. He knows how to handle 'em better than I do. Yore pardner is with the B Arrow gang and Eddie Grimes, and if I was you I'd get him away from 'em. Shorty Gallup got whipped by Frank Judd, and Eddie got fired by Shorty; so there might be some fireworks, if they get a few more drinks."

"Sleepy can take care of himself," smiled Hashknife.

"I s'pose he can."

The sheriff went back to his office and Hashknife sauntered over to Cooper's store, where he stood on the sidewalk for a while. He saw Oscar Johnson ride in and go to the office. It was dark now. After smoking a cigarette, Hashknife strolled down the street and went up to his room, where he sat down and tried to get interested in an old magazine, but without any success.

Then he decided to go down and talk with Ma Cooper and Marion. He didn't want to mix with the men in the Stormy River saloon, because he didn't want to have any trouble with Shorty, who very likely had not forgotten what had taken place at the TD corral that day.

But he did not find any one at home at the Cooper house; so he sprawled in a deep porch chair to wait for them to return. He decided that they had gone up to the store, and would return in a short time.

He smoked a cigarette and went to sleep, stretched out in the big chair. Suddenly he awoke, staring at the ceiling of the porch; wondering where he was. There were voices close to him; the voices of a man and a woman. He could not see them, because they were on the other side of the porch railing, but he could hear them plainly. It was Marion talking to Tex Blanco.

Hashknife did not want to listen, but after a few words he decided to stay where he was. Marion was saying: —

"You shouldn't have walked down here with me."

"I suppose not, Marion. Yes, I'm goin' to call you Marion. I call you that to myself all the time. I heard a preacher say it is just as bad to think profanity as it is to speak it; so if I think Marion, I'll say Marion."

"That part is all right," she said slowly.

"That's fine. Gee, it's been a tough week for me — havin' to give up takin' Jimmy to school."

"It was the best thing to do, Mr. Blanco."

"Won't yuh call me Tex? My right name is Bryan. They even mixed my names — Irish and Spanish. Nobody ever calls me Bryan; not even my mother, and she named me. I wish you could meet her. We talk about you a lot."

"I — I don't know why you should, Tex."

"Why? Lord love yuh, Marion — why shouldn't we? Don't go in the house, please. Stay here and talk to me."

"Oh, I don't know —" faltered Marion. "You know how they feel about you, Tex. If any one knew I was here with you, I'd lose my school. I may lose it anyway. It isn't me — it's just the way things are, don't you see?"

"What does the school amount to, if you say it isn't you? Marion, you've got to listen to me. I've got to tell you right now. The rest of the world can go hang. I —"

"Don't, Tex! Oh, can't you see it is no use?"

"No, I can't" said Tex slowly. "I can't see — unless you believe what folks have told yuh, Marion. They have been my judges for a long time. They must be without sin, because they throw rocks all the time.

"I'm no saint. Oh, I know what they say about me. They have probably told yuh I killed Buck Dennig, because he accused me of cheating; and they can't arrest me because there's no evidence. They've put a lot of their crimes on me. And it never made much difference — until you came along.

"I ought to understand how you feel, Marion. But I guess I'm kinda dumb. I couldn't expect you to marry a man of my reputation — unless yuh knew it wasn't true — and I can't prove my innocence. They can't prove me guilty and I can't prove my innocence."

"Tex," said Marion softly, "would you swear to me that you are innocent of any crime?"

"Of any crime they accuse me — yes, Marion."

"Even of holding up that stage the other day?"

Marion's voice was pitched so low that Hashknife had to strain his ears to hear her.

Tex laughed softly. "Bless yore heart — of course I swear it."

"Oh, I'm sorry, Tex; so sorry I don't know what to say."

"Sorry? Because I denied doin' it, Marion?"

"Because that day — oh, don't you understand? Ma Cooper and I saw that hold-up. We were on the mesa. And after it was all over, I — I found your revolver — the one with the pearl handle."

"You found it?" Tex's voice was hoarse.

"It's in my trunk, Tex. Ma Cooper knows. We'll never tell anybody, Tex. Good-bye."

She came slowly up the steps and went into the house, passing within six feet of Hashknife, who hunched lower in the big chair, thankful to be overlooked. He heard Tex walking slowly away, his spurs rasping on the sidewalk. Hashknife got to his feet and stepped off the porch. He decided not to wait for Mrs. Cooper to come back, but met her just outside the gate.

"This is Hartley, Mrs. Cooper," he said. "Dropped in to see yuh, didn't find anybody at home, and went to sleep on the porch."

Mrs. Cooper laughed shortly. "Wasn't Miss Evans at home?"

"She came a few minutes ago."

"I see. Hootie said for me to tell yuh to run in and see him, if I seen yuh."

"All right. Good-night, Mrs. Cooper."

Hashknife walked up to the store, where he found Hootie waiting on some customers. As soon as Hootie was at liberty, he motioned for Hashknife to meet him at the rear of the store.

"I just wanted to let yuh know that the sheriff sent a telegram yesterday to my brother in Mizpa, Arizona, askin' him what he knew about you, Hartley."

"Yea-a-ah?" drawled Hashknife, not knowing what else to say.

"And Oscar, his deputy, brought back a wire from Jim this evenin'. It said, "Never knew anybody by the name of Hashknife Hartley in my life'."

"Well," said Hashknife, after a short pause, "that's kinda queer, don'tcha think, Mr. Cooper?"

"I thought it was," dryly. "That's why I told yuh."

He moved away to wait on another customer, and Hashknife sauntered outside.

"Next time I start lyin', I'll pick a town that ain't on no map," he told himself, grinning in spite of the fact that he had been caught in the lie. "But just why would the sheriff go to all that trouble and expense. Mebby I better go down and see him."

Hashknife went to the office, where he found Oscar Johnson sprawled in a chair. The tall, sad-faced deputy looked at Hashknife with a funereal expression, a cigarette hanging loosely from the corner of his mouth.

"Got a letter for yuh, Hartley," he said, waving one limp hand toward the sheriff's desk. "'S over there."

Hashknife picked up the letter and glanced at the post mark. It had been posted in Garnet, and sent to him in care of the sheriff's office. He tore one end off the envelope and drew out the enclosure. It read:

"We will give you eight hours to leave this valley.
"THE BUNCH."

It was identical with the letter Sears, the detective, had received. Hashknife glanced sharply at Oscar, who was looking at him quizzically. The sheriff came in, stopped short and looked at Hashknife, who smiled and held out the warning for his inspection.

The sheriff scowled at the message for a moment, and went to his desk, where he secured the note which had been sent to Sears, and compared the writing. It was identical.

"Just alike, eh?" asked Hashknife.

"Exactly."

"But what does it mean? Who is the Bunch?"

"That's what Sears wondered."

"Why do they want me out of the valley?"

The sheriff walked over and closed the door, as though he did not want anybody else to hear what he was going to say. He came back to his desk and faced Hashknife.

"I dunno why they want yuh out, Hartley," he said. "You two fellers have had me kinda guessin', don'tcha know it? I'm goin' to put my cards on the table. You told folks that you came over the divide from Piney Lake, didn't yuh?

"Well, you didn't, Hartley. Alex McLean saw yuh leave Wallgate, and yuh couldn't have made the trip to Piney Lake and back here in that length of time. You told Hootie Cooper that you knowed Jim Cooper in Mizpa, Arizona. And" — he reached in his pocket and drew out a telegram — "this is his reply."

"I've heard it," said Hashknife calmly. "Hootie told me about it."

"Jim Cooper never met yuh in his life."

"Not to my knowledge, Sheriff."

"Then why didja —"

"Lie?" Hashknife smiled. "Oh, I dunno. Force of habit, I suppose. Any other charges?"

"No-o-o, I don't reckon so."

"All right; I'm guilty on both counts. What's the penalty for lyin' in this county?"

The sheriff put the telegram in his pocket. For all his trouble he was no better off than before.

"I reckon there ain't no penalty," he said slowly. "But it kinda makes a feller lose faith in yuh."

"Oh, yea-a-ah," drawled Hashknife. "As a matter of fact, you didn't have no faith in me to start with, Sheriff. If yuh had, you'd have swallered my lies instead of provin' me a liar. Now that you've proved it, what are yuh goin' to do about it?"

The sheriff rubbed his nose thoughtfully. "Nothin' I guess."

He sat down in his desk-chair and filled an old pipe. Oscar grinned softly and winked at Hashknife.

"You don't need to wink at anybody," said the sheriff. "It was yore idea — this investigation, Oscar."

"Well, I sink along with yuh, don't I? I'm not howlin' about it. As a detective, I'm a hell of a good night herder. I reckon Hartley ain't the first puncher that ever told a lie, and I ain't lost no faith in him. He didn't hedge none, did he? Admitted that we had the goods on him, Pat. He could have sworn that he had a different name when he knowed Jim Cooper — and he could have sworn that Alex McLean was a damn liar, which he is most of the time."

"I thought of both," said Hashknife. "But what's the use? I never knew Jim Cooper. The sign on his store blew down one afternoon and almost crowned me. And we did not come from Piney Lake."

"Why didja say yuh came from Piney Lake?" asked the sheriff.

"Thought it might be a good place to be from."

"I reckon that's a good answer, Hartley, if that's yore name."

"You'd have a hell of a time provin' it isn't."

Hashknife walked over to the door, opened it and stood there, looking up the street. Over at the Stormy River saloon hitch-rack, a cowboy was singing at the top of his voice. Came the rasp of shod hoofs against the hard street, a shrill yell, a fusillade of revolver shots, sparking upward.

The sheriff came quickly to the doorway.

"Happy punchers goin' home," laughed Hashknife.

"Dang fools!" snorted the sheriff. "Liable to hurt somebody, shootin' wild thataway."

Some one was coming down the sidewalk toward the office. It was Sleepy, grinning widely.

"Well, they all got away without hurtin' anybody," he said. "Them last two was Shorty Gallup and Matt Sturgis, boiled drunk."

Sleepy leaned against the wall and rolled a cigarette.

"Thought for a while there was goin' to be trouble. The TD gang wanted to act bad. Gallup sent word to Judd, of the B Arrow, that he was goin' to get him. Severn and McLean tried to talk him out of it, but he wouldn't listen; so McLean and Severn went home.

"Judd was all set to swap lead with Shorty, but Grimes and Corbett talked him out of the notion. I helped a little, I suppose. Anyway, the B Arrow gang pulled out, and when Shorty heard about it he sang a song, piled on his bronc and shot a few holes in the sky."

"I'll bet he was glad Judd pulled out," said Oscar. "Pat wanted me to go over and ride herd on 'em, but I told him I wouldn't do it. Let 'em fight it out. If they've got it in their system — let 'em fight."

"You was scared to go over," growled Pat.

"You didn't go, didja?" queried Oscar. "When I refused — why didn't you do it. Don't talk to me about bein' scared."

"They didn't start nothin' with you, did they. Sleepy?" asked Hashknife.

"Nothin' but talk. This McLean person came up to me in the Stormy River, and he — he's pretty well loaded — and he stuck his — face into mine, and he said, 'I know somethin' about you.'

"I kicked his feet out from under him and he sets down on the bar rail like a ton of bricks. I reckon it was quite a shock, because when he got to his feet again, he's kinda puckered up, and I asked him what he knows.

"But he didn't say. He went out of there kinda bent in the shape of a chair; but I guess he got straightened out to ride a horse."

Oscar laughed immoderately, but the sheriff was serious. He knew what McLean meant.

"We've been exposed," smiled Hashknife. "They all know we didn't come from Piney Lake, and they know I never met Jim Cooper."

Sleepy's mouth sagged for a moment, as he hooked his thumbs over the waist-band of his pants, staring at the sheriff and the deputy.

"Well," he said softly, "what's the next thing to do, Hashknife?"

"Go to bed, I suppose," grinned Hashknife. "Goodnight, officers."

They went up the street together and entered the hotel room, where Hashknife told Sleepy all about their exposure, as liars of the first vintage, and also showed him the warning note. Sleepy whistled through his teeth and essayed a clumsy clog in the middle of the floor.

"Must please you, don't it?" asked Hashknife.

"Gives me a talkin' point, any old time you accuse me of stretchin' things," laughed Sleepy.

"What do yuh think of the note?"

"Scares me to death."

"It's serious, Sleepy."

"So am I. In the mornin' I'm goin' down and make my peace with Ma Cooper and Miss Evans. If I have to, I'll tell 'em I met you after you was in Mizpa. Yuh see, I never pretended to know Jim Cooper."

Sleepy laughed gleefully. "And I saw Tex Blanco tonight. They can say what they want to about him, he can take care of himself. I was almost tempted to shoot him and steal his shirt. Man, what a garment! I wonder if Miss Evans is goin' to marry him."

"I don't think so, Sleepy."

"*You* don't think so? Is that an official count of all the votes, Hashknife?"

Hashknife shook his head slowly. "There may be a few counties to hear from yet, Sleepy. We better hit the hay, because we've only got eight hours left."

"When do we run, Hashknife?"

Hashknife considered his two boots thoughtfully.

"Just as soon as we find somebody to run after."

Mrs. Blanco, Tex's mother, was a little old Irish woman, not over sixty years of age, but looking much older. Her hair was as white as snow, her face deeply lined and tanned. Her name had been Mary Bryan before she married Enrique Blanco, down in the Rio Grande, and in her voice was still the brogue of old Wexford.

This early morning she stood in the kitchen door at the B Arrow, an anxious expression in her blue eyes. Leaning against the wall beside her was Andy Hastings, his hands shoved deeply in his pockets, hair uncombed, a stubble of whiskers on his lean jaw.

"Yuh think he's sick bad?" asked Andy.

"Aye, he's bad, Andy. High fever. Well, ye saw the lad. Tex is in there with him now. I think ye better saddle and get the doctor, Andy."

"Sure, I'll do that."

Andy went striding down to the stable, and in a few moments Tex came out and stood beside his mother.

"Sleepin'," he said softly. "Is Andy goin' for the doctor, mother?"

"Aye."

"He's a sick boy," said Tex slowly. "He didn't know me."

"It's the fever. Children get it bad. And they get over it quick. They can stand more than a grown-up."

"He was talkin' about the school, mother; askin' for Miss Evans; wantin' to fight the Beebee boy. I thought he looked kinda bad when Andy brought him home last night."

"Aye; it was growin' on him then, Tex. But mebby it is only an upset stummick after all. Children get those things."

Andy Hastings led his horse from the stable, mounted and rode out through the big gate, forgetting to wear a hat.

"He thinks a world of the lad," said Mrs. Blanco.

"We all do, mother. I'd rather lose my right hand than —" Tex turned and went back in the house. The old lady nodded her head slowly.

Kit Carson, Tommy Corbett and Frank Judd were coming up from the bunk-house, ready for breakfast, and she told them about little Jimmy being sick.

"Gee, that's tough," said Judd. "Andy went after a doctor, didn't he?"

"Why didn't he send one of us?" asked Tommy. "He should have stayed with Jimmy. Where's Tex?"

"He's in there with Jimmy. Ye'll have to wait a while for breakfast, boys; I haven't started it yet."

"That's all right, Mother Blanco," said Judd quickly. "You jist take yore time. There's nothin' we've got to do early this mornin', anyway. Can we do anythin' for Jimmy?"

"Not a thing, Frank. I'll get breakfast now."

Andy Hastings did not spare his horse, and it was still early morning when he rode up to the doctor's house in Pineville. Old Doctor Brent answered his summons, and promised to start for the ranch as soon as he could dress and get his horse and buggy.

Andy rode back up the street and went to Cooper's home, where he found them at breakfast.

"I jist wanted to see Miss Evans," said Andy to Ma Cooper.

Marion came to the door and Andy told her about Jimmy.

"I jist wanted yuh to know why he didn't show up at the school," he told her.

"Is he very sick?" asked Marion anxiously.

"Yes'm, I reckon he's pretty bad. Mother Blanco and Tex was up with him most all night. They didn't tell me until this mornin'; so I came right away for the doctor. He's kinda out of his head, yuh see."

Andy squinted painfully. "He didn't know me; didn't know Tex either. Jist talked about the school and you, ma'am. And he wanted to fight the Beebee boy." Andy turned his head away. "He's quite a fighter, ma'am — Jimmy is. He thinks yo're pretty fine. He talked about you goin' away."

Andy turned and looked at Marion. "You ain't goin' away, are yuh?"

"I hope not, Mr. Hastings."

"I hope not m'self. Jimmy's learnin' so fast. Well, I've got to git back to the ranch."

"Is there anythin' we can do, Andy?" asked Ma Cooper.

"Not a thing, thank yuh, Mrs. Cooper."

"Will he be nursed all right out there?" asked Marion.

"Oh, shore. Mother Blanco is fine thataway. I'll let yuh know how he comes along."

Andy rode back to the main street, where he met the doctor, and they went to the ranch together.

Marion had been greatly worried ever since Mrs. Cooper had told her of meeting Hashknife at the gate, and that Hashknife said he had been asleep on the porch. Marion remembered that she and Tex had stood near the porch, and she was afraid that Hashknife had heard what she told Tex about finding that gun. Marion did not tell Ma Cooper that she had told Tex.

Hashknife cautioned Sleepy that morning. He did not know just how much of that note was pure bluff, and even if it was part bluff, they were taking a big chance in staying around Pineville.

They met the sheriff after breakfast, and he seemed a little surprised to meet them.

"Yo're eight hours are up," he told Hashknife.

"We realize that," smiled Hashknife. "But it's daylight; and that bunch don't work in daylight."

"Yo're just guessin', ain'tcha?"

Hashknife studied the sheriff seriously. "You ain't tryin' to run us out, are yuh, Sheriff?"

"No, I'm not. I don't sabe yuh, though."

"Yuh don't need to. What yuh don't know won't hurt yuh."

"Mm-m-m. Well, go ahead and get killed, if yuh feel thataway."

"No, that ain't the idea, Sheriff. Don't go off half-cocked. You've been tryin' to put the deadwood on us ever since we came here. You proved me a liar, didn't yuh? Oh, that's all right. Let's drop it and be friends."

Pat Lynch looked quizzically at Hashknife. "I reckon I might as well, Hartley. Me and Oscar argued a lot about you two fellers, and he stuck up for yuh. I swear I don't know a thing about yuh, except that yuh lied — and admitted it like a gentleman."

"Well, that's settled," grinned Hashknife, taking the note from his pocket. "Who wrote that, Sheriff?"

"I don't know," declared the sheriff. "It's the same writin' as was on the other note."

"Can you get hold of a sample of Tex Blanco's writin'?"

The sheriff blinked quickly and shifted his eyes toward the bank building across the street.

"Why do yuh want a sample of his writin', Hartley?"

"You wouldn't have to be very bright to answer that yourself, Sheriff."

"Uh-huh."

The sheriff shifted uneasily for a moment. Then:

"Hartley, I don't want this to go any further, because Heffner says it don't prove nothin'; but we compared the other note with Blanco' signature at the bank, and the B in Bunch is the same as the B in Blanco."

"Why does Heffner say it doesn't prove anythin'?"

"Says it would take an expert to prove it. And even at that a cow jury prob'ly wouldn't believe it. But the B is the same, Hartley. It's got the curlycue at the bottom and one at the top. I'm no expert, but I could see that. But don't say anythin', Hartley."

"I'm not sayin' anythin', Sheriff; but I'd like to see that signature."

"I'll get it for yuh, as soon as the bank opens."

The sheriff glanced at his watch.

"Tex Blanco quarrelled with Buck Dennig the night Dennig was killed, didn't he?" asked Hashknife.

"Dennig accused him of cheatin' at poker," said the sheriff. "But that an't evidence. Somebody stole the ten thousand off Buck that night, but we've no trace of that. Buck cashed a cheque for it that afternoon. Nobody knows what he was goin' to do with the money. Might as well go over to the bank and get that signature; it's ten o'clock."

They went over and started into the bank, but found the door locked. The sheriff looked at his watch again.

"My watch must be fast," he said, winding it slowly. Hashknife looked at his watch, which showed ten minutes after ten.

"Shearer's late," decided the Sheriff, and they sat down on the edge of the high sidewalk to wait.

They saw Tex Blanco ride in and go to the little drug store down the street. He came out in a few moments, mounted and rode swiftly out of town. Hootie Cooper came along, tried the bank door, and came out to the edge of the sidewalk.

"Shearer must have overslept," he said.

But Guy Shearer, the cashier, did not come. Several other people tried to get into the bank. It was after ten-thirty, when old John Rice, president of the bank, came along. He and Shearer were the only employees of the bank, and Rice was not in the habit of coming very early. Rice was a small, gray-haired man, slightly crippled, an old timer in the Stormy River country.

He seemed greatly surprised to find the bank still closed.

"Perhaps Guy is sick," he said, as he unlocked the front door. "He was all right yesterday. Come right in, gentlemen."

They followed him in. He carefully blocked the door open, before doing anything else. The Pineville bank was a small institution; the room being about twenty by thirty feet in size, less than a third of it used for office space.

Rice led the way to the low railing, which separated the office desks from the rest of the building, swung open the gate and stepped inside. At the rear of this was the front of the vault, which was little more than a large safe, set into the wall. Rice placed his hat on a desk and started to turn back to the men, when he stopped and leaned forward, both hands on the desk.

"My God!" he exclaimed loudly. "What has been done here?"

Hashknife had halted near the gate, and now he flung it open and stepped inside, with the sheriff close behind him.

CHAPTER NINE

Stretched out on the floor, half under the desk, was Guy Shearer, the cashier, his head in a pool of blood. On the floor near him was a length of lariat rope. Hashknife took one look at Shearer and decided he was dead. Quickly the sheriff and Rice dropped on their knees beside him, while Hootie and Sleepy leaned across the railing and watched them turn the man over on his back.

Hashknife picked up the rope, looked it over quickly. It was an ordinary spot-cord rope, which had been used quite a lot. He inspected both ends of the rope quickly. One end had been wrapped tightly with a fine copper wire, while the other end, frayed slightly, showed a fresh cut.

Hashknife moved around the room, glancing sharply from one corner to another, holding the rope in one hand. The men were too interested in the dead cashier to pay any attention to Hashknife. Suddenly he stooped and picked up an object from near the leg of the desk, concealing it in his hand for a few moments, while he played idly with the rope, and then slipping it into his pocket.

"There's no use goin' for the doctor," Hootie was saying. "He's gone out to the B Arrow to see Hastings' kid."

John Rice's face was very white and his lips trembled as he leaned against the railing and looked at the dead cashier.

"You better set down, John," advised the sheriff. "There ain't no use of yuh standin' up. Nothin' yuh can do. He's as dead as a salt herrin'."

"But why — who killed him, Pat? The door was locked."

The old banker looked around the room and his gaze came back to the vault door.

"Those windows won't open," he said slowly. "Will some of you lock the front door? We can't have folks coming in here now."

Sleepy walked over and closed the door.

"If I were in yore place," said Hashknife, "I'd open the vault and have a look inside."

"But the vault is locked," said Rice. "Nobody could —"

"Folks don't usually break into a bank just to kill the cashier, yuh know."

"Mebby yuh better, John," said the sheriff.

The old man went over to the vault and slowly worked the combination. None of the men went near him. He swung the door open, and after a moment of inspection, stepped back.

"It — it has been cleaned out," he said painfully.

Hashknife and the sheriff walked over beside him. The inside door was partly open. The sheriff swung it the rest of the way, disclosing an empty interior. That door opened with a key, and there was no key in the lock.

"Better close it up," said Hashknife. "No use tellin' everybody."

Rice closed the outer door, and turned the combination.

"This is terrible," said Rice hoarsely. "What can we do?"

The sheriff shook his head helplessly, staring at the body of the cashier. Sleepy perched on the rail, smoking a cigarette, keeping an eye on Hashknife, who was idly swinging the rope in his hand. The sheriff took the rope and looked at it. "This was on the floor, wasn't it, Hartley?"

"Yeah," said Hashknife. He turned to Rice. "Was the cashier in the habit of workin' in here at night?"

"Not very often. There wasn't enough work for that."

"Uh-huh. He had a key to the inside door of that vault?"

"Oh, certainly."

"Let's see if he's still got it. Shall I search him, or will you, sheriff?"

"You do it," said the sheriff.

In a trouser pocket Hashknife found the keyring, and Rice identified the key.

"Did anybody, except you two, know the combination?"

"Just the two of us," said Rice wearily.

Hashknife and the sheriff walked around the place. There was no evidence that any one had been at work.

The desks were orderly. Hashknife went back and examined the body. The blow had been struck from behind, and might have been made with the barrel of a heavy revolver.

"What do yuh think, Hartley?" asked the sheriff.

"Hard to tell. Looks as though somebody had met this man, forced him here at the point of a gun, robbed the vault and then hit him over the head. They went through the front door, which is on a spring lock. Mebby they intended to just tie him up on here, but somethin' happened and they killed him, and forgot their rope."

"That's my theory too!" exclaimed the sheriff. "That's what they done. Prob'ly met Shearer on the street. Mebby he recognized them, and they had to kill him."

"That sounds reasonable," agreed Hashknife. He turned to Rice. "Did they get much from the vault?"

"At least twenty-five thousand dollars."

Hashknife whistled softly. "I didn't know yuh kept that much cash in a bank of this size."

"Sometimes more than that. We won't know until a check is made of it."

"I hate to move that body until the coroner gets here," said the sheriff. "He ought to be back in a little while. I think I'll go down to Allen's place and see what they know about Shearer. Allen's place is where Shearer lived," he explained to Hashknife. "Want to walk down?"

"Yeah, I'll go with yuh."

"I'd like to have one of you stay here with me," said Rice quickly.

"I'll stay," said Sleepy. "I'm good company."

They walked down to the house and inquired of Mrs. Allen, but did not tell her that Shearer was dead, until she said that Shearer did not show up for breakfast. She did not know whether he had left early or late the evening before, as he had a room on the lower floor, with an outside entrance.

She was greatly shocked to know that he was dead, and let them in to examine his room. The bed had not been disturbed. On the dresser was an enlargement from a snapshot picture, showing the front of the bank, Shearer, Buck Dennig, Cleve Tolman and John Rice.

"That picture was taken about the time Shearer went to work for the bank," said the sheriff. "He was with the Garnet Mercantile Company for quite a while before he came here. That's Buck Dennig next to Shearer."

"Buck was a good-lookin' feller," said Hashknife.

"And a nice feller too. Well, I guess we'll have to go back and wait for Doc Brent to come back from the B Arrow. This will shore upset this town."

They went back up the street. Quite a crowd had collected in front of the bank, and as they drew near to the bank, old Doctor Brent drove in from the east side of the town. Some one told him about the trouble at the bank, and he stopped at the little hitch-rack. The sheriff went in with him, but Hashknife stayed outside, listening to the different opinions. Hootie was telling them all about the discovery of the murder.

Cleve Tolman rode in. He was a director in the bank and one of the heaviest depositors. Hashknife watched him go in. In a few minutes some of the men secured a narrow cot, which they used as a stretcher to carry the body down to the doctor's office; and the bank closed its door for the day.

The crowd dispersed quickly after the body had been taken away. Sleepy joined Hashknife and they sat on the edge of the sidewalk together.

"I suppose that's the work of the Bunch," said Sleepy.

"Looks thataway," nodded Hashknife.

Sleepy looked around, as he rolled a cigarette, edged a little closer to Hashknife, and said: —

"What did yuh find in there, Hashknife?"

"You saw me find it?"

"Yeah. Nobody else did, though."

Hashknife reached in his pocket and drew out a hondoo, the loop on the end of a lariat, through which the rope runs. It was of metal, covered with leather, and in the leather had been burned the initial B and a crudely drawn arrow; the mark of the B Arrow Ranch.

Sleepy examined it closely and gave it back to Hashknife.

"Cut it off the rope and then lost it, eh?"

Hashknife nodded slowly, as he put the hondoo in his pocket.

"Looks thataway. They meant to tie Shearer, and didn't want that marked hondoo to be found. Probably workin' in the dark, and lost it. That hondoo might hang somebody, Sleepy."

"Shore as hell. Ain't yuh goin' to give it the sheriff?"

"Not yet. There's several men at the B Arrow, and they didn't all kill Shearer."

"They must be the Bunch," said Sleepy quietly. "We'll have to keep an eye on 'em, cowboy. I hear they've been rustlin' TD beef for a long time. But I like Judd and Corbett. Carson don't say much. They tell me Judd is a fighter. He whipped hell out of Shorty Gallup."

"So did Grimes," smiled Hashknife. "He had Shorty whipped that day we met him. It was Sturgis who knocked Grimes down, yuh remember — hit him from behind."

"Yeah, that's right. This killin' will make folks sore. This Shearer was well liked."

Oscar Johnson came along and sat down with them.

"Lotsa crime around here," he said. "I liked Shearer. Who do you suppose killed him, Hartley?"

"The same folks who sent us that note, Johnson."

"I s'pose. Pat was surprised that you fellers didn't pull out. Yore eight hours are up long ago."

"I dunno," mused Hashknife. "Eight hours from when? They should have set a time, Oscar. How would they know when I got that note?"

"That's right. But you wouldn't go, anyway. I told Pat you had more nerve than Sears did. He shore high-tailed quick. I never seen a cow detective yet that had any nerve. We've got a job on our hands, tryin' to clear all this up. Don't think we ever will. Takes brains, don'tcha know it. Me and Pat ain't got enough. He thinks he's smart; but I know him."

"Don't yuh even suspect anybody?" asked Sleepy.

"Shore," nodded Oscar solemnly. "But what's the use? Yuh can't prove it. Look at the money they've got! Ten thousand from Buck Dennig, three thousand from that stage, and now they get about twenty-five thousand more. Thirty-eight thousand dollars!"

"And two dead men," said Hashknife.

"Yeah — two dead men. That kind of money ought to burn a man, Hartley."

"It will."

"Mebby. If we don't never catch 'em, it won't."

"Who was sick at the B Arrow this mornin'?"

"Little Jimmy Hastings. Tex came in after medicine. Told me the doctor was scared the kid had typhoid. Tex thinks a lot of that kid. He's a queer feller, this Tex Blanco. You wasn't here the day the stage was held up, was yuh? No, that was before yuh came. Me and Pat went out to where the stage was robbed. Mrs. Cooper and Miss Evans had been to Garnet, and they must have been pretty close behind the stage.

"We found where the robbery had been pulled off, and we saw where Cooper's buckboard had pulled out of the road at the same spot. And we found a woman's tracks, where she left the buckboard and walked about four or five steps and then came back.

"But them women wouldn't admit that they seen the hold-up, nor that they walked around at the spot. Pat's got an idea that they're keepin' somethin' quiet. Anyway, we came back past the B Arrow and talked with Andy Hastings. He said that Tex went to Garnet to the dance the night before.

"And, while we was talkin' to Andy, Tex rode in. He shore looked tough. There was blood on his muffler and on his shirt, and he wore his hat tilted to one side, as though to hide somethin'. And another thing — he didn't have no gun in his holster. Jist nodded howdy to us and rode on. Acted as though he didn't want to talk with us. It shore looked queer to me."

"Why didn't yuh ask him where he'd been?" asked Hashknife.

"Yea-a-ah! In the first place, it wasn't none of our dang business."

"Wasn't Buck Dennig killed in the same way as Shearer?"

"Shore was. I never thought of that."

"And they tell me that Windy March, the stage driver, never saw the men who held him up."

"That's right, Hartley. Oh, they're clever all right. Poor Windy ain't over it yet. He sat there and looked the way they wanted him to look. I don't blame him m'self."

"Neither do I," said Hashknife seriously. "Did any of yuh check up on Tex, to see if he *was* at Garnet that night?"

"I don't guess anybody did, Hartley."

"And yuh don't know what Buck Dennig was goin' to do with that ten thousand?"

"Nope; never knew he had it until after he was killed."

"I guess we better go and eat, before yuh admit that yuh ain't done a thing."

"Hell, I can admit that on an empty stummick — but I'll eat with yuh."

> "Ro-o-ho-oll on, Silv'ry Moo-on,
> Light the trav'ler on his wayha-a-ay,
> O, la-lay-hee-e-e, O, la-lay-he-hoo-o-o-o."

As a yodler, Luke Jones, cook for the TD outfit, was terrible. In fact, it was a series of broken notes, wails and hoots, sent forth at the top of his voice, as he leaned against the side of the kitchen door. In his left hand he held a tin cup, which contained some violet-tinted liquid, while his right hand, concealed beneath his dirty apron, gripped a big single-action Colt revolver.

Luke was very drunk, but very much awake. His bleared eyes caught sight of what appeared to be the brim of a sombrero, extending just out from the corner of the bunk-house. He jerked his hand from beneath the apron and fired from his hip. The bullet smashed a window in the bunk-house, three feet from the corner, and old Luke grinned, exposing a few crooked teeth. He drank from the cup, twisted his face in a scowl and yelled: —

"C'mon out and git shot, you chuckwalla!"

But no one came out. Luke had been there for fifteen minutes, defying the whole TD outfit. Shorty Gallup had kicked on the breakfast, as well he might, because Luke was drunk when he cooked it; drunk on prune whisky, which he had made himself. Luke was a periodical drunkard, but he had always gone to town to celebrate.

And Luke had taken Shorty's kicks as personal insults. He wanted to show them who was boss of that kitchen — and he was doing it. He had Shorty, Matt Sturgis, Alex McLean and Bud Hough hiding out behind the bunkhouse. Tolman and Dobe Severn had left for town before Luke's outburst.

"I'm goin' to step out and kill that old fool," declared Shorty angrily. "He deserves it, I tell yuh. Aw, he couldn't hit me, even if he had a shotgun. My God, there goes another window!"

Shorty drew his gun and stepped out quickly from the side of the bunk-house. Came a sharp "whap!" something went "pwee-e-e," down toward the corral, and Shorty fell back against the wall, swearing softly.

"Look at that!" he wailed, indicating the right leg of his bat-wing chaps, where a bullet had torn away the leather and forcibly removed one of Shorty's silver rosettes. It was the rosette they heard pweeing its way down past the corral.

"Couldn't hit yuh without a shot-gun," jeered Bud Hough.

"Accident — mebby," said Matt Sturgis.

"Mebby," said Shorty dryly. "Peek around there and see what he's doin', Alex."

"When I'm too old to be of any use," grinned Alex. "You do yore own peekin'."

They did not know Luke had gone in the kitchen and filled his tin cup again, and was now sitting on the steps. The home-made liquor had made his legs unstable. He had two more shells in his gun; so he fired both of them at the door of the bunk-house. One struck the roof of the stable and the other hit the ground half-way between Luke and the bunk-house, and ricochetted its way off across the hills.

But the boys behind the bunk-house stayed where they were for about fifteen minutes more, before Shorty mustered up nerve enough to peek around the corner again. Only the soles of Luke's boots were visible, sticking through the kitchen doorway.

They surrounded the recumbent form of the old cook, took the gun from his unresisting hand, and told him what they thought of him. But it was all right with old Luke Jones; he couldn't hear them.

"Hitch up the buckboard, Bud," ordered Shorty. "We're goin' to ship him away from here right now. When he wakes up, he won't be the TD cook any longer."

So they took old Luke to Pineville, along with all his possessions and left him at the livery stable to sleep off his prune juice distillation. McLean and Bud Hough brought him to town, where they met Tolman and told him what Luke had done.

Tolman didn't like the idea of losing a cook, but he said nothing. Tolman was upset over the killing of Shearer and the robbery of the bank. Being a director and a heavy depositor, he was naturally much concerned.

Hashknife and Sleepy were with Oscar Johnson when the stage came in that afternoon, and they noticed that

Windy had a passenger; a middle-aged, thin-faced man, who wore glasses and was dressed in a rusty black suit.

The passenger met Sam Hall and old man Beebee, and the three of them walked out to the schoolhouse. It was almost four o'clock when they came; so they waited until Marion dismissed school.

When the last pupil had left the room they walked in. Marion looked at them wonderingly, but she did not have to wait long for an explanation.

"Miss Evans, this here is Mr. Long," said Sam Hall, in his nasal drawl. "Mr. Long teached the school about a month last term, when our reg'lar teacher quit. Now, we've been thinkin' it over pretty strong, and we come to the conclusion that this here ain't no job for a lady; so we've done hired Mr. Long to take over the school."

Marion gasped. "You mean — to take my position?"

"Yes'm," said Beebee firmly. "That's the idea, ma'am. He will begin teachin' tomorrow mornin'."

"But such a thing is unheard of," protested Marion. "You told me I was to have the school for this term."

"Yeah, we did think so. But you — well, you ain't been so satisfactory, ma'am. A lot of the wimmin' ain't satisfied, yuh see."

"So the women run the school, instead of the trustees."

"We don't want no hard feelin's," said Sam Hall quickly.

In a dazed sort of way Marion gathered up her belongings and left the school-house, while Beebee, Hall and the new teacher waited for her to go. She did not tell them good-bye.

"Pers'nally," said Sam Hall, after Marion had gone, "I think she's so darn pretty that the wimmin' got jealous."

"A paragon of pulchritude," said Long seriously.

"I been tryin' to think of that," said Beebee.

"You have, like hell!" snorted Sam Hall. "The only big word you know is asafedita; and yuh only know that because yuh wear it in a bag, hanging around yore neck to keep away disease."

Marion went straight home, heartsick over her dismissal, wondering what to do next. There was no one at home; so she dumped her books on the porch and sat down to try to adjust her thoughts. That noon she had heard of the bank robbery and murder of the cashier, but all that had faded to insignificance now.

She was so deep in her own thoughts that she did not see Andy Hastings ride up to the gate in the B Arrow buckboard and tie his team, nor did she look up until he was standing at the bottom of the steps, hat in hand.

"I came past the school-house," he told her. "Old man Beebee told me you wasn't there no more; so I came here to find yuh, ma'am."

Mrs. Cooper came to the gate, looked curiously at the team, and came on up the walk. Andy glanced at her, but turned back to Marion.

"I didn't have much hopes," he confessed slowly, as Ma Cooper halted beside him, looking inquiringly at Marion.

"I talked it over with Tex, and he said yuh wouldn't come. But jist the same I hitched up the buckboard."

"I don't understand," said Marion blankly.

"It's Jimmy — the little feller, ma'am. He's got typhoid, the doctor says. He keeps callin' for you all the time. He don't know none of us, ma'am; jist wants you."

"That's yore little boy, Andy?" asked Ma Cooper.

"Yes'm — my boy."

"But Marion can't go out there, Andy. She's got her school."

Marion lifted her eyes and looked at Ma Cooper.

"I've lost the school, Ma. A man — a Mr. Long from Garnet, has been hired to take my place."

"Oh, yuh don't mean that, Marion?"

"Old Beebee told me," said Andy.

"Yes, it's a fact," said Marion slowly. "They were not satisfied with my work."

Andy sighed and adjusted the band on his hat. "I'm sorry yuh can't go, ma'am. Mebby he'll be all right. I jist thought mebby yuh — thank yuh jist the same."

He started away, but Marion stopped him.

"I guess I'll go," she said. "It — it don't make so much difference now."

"That's the stuff!" exclaimed Ma Cooper. "You jist go. If a lot of these Pineville fork-tongues want to talk — let 'em talk. Wait'll I meet old lady Beebee and Hall. You jist go, Honey. If you want to stay all night — you stay. I'll come out tomorrow myself. You jist grab a night-gown, and go."

Ma Cooper fairly shooed her out to the buckboard and helped her climb in. Andy was so excited that he almost upset the buckboard.

"Don't go the back way!" yelled Ma Cooper. "Go down the main street. Give 'em all a chance to talk."

And they did go down the main street, with the buckskin team on the run, and Marion clinging to her hat with one hand and the seat with the other. They almost ran over old man Beebee and Sam Hall, who were a bit slow at getting out of the road.

"Looks to me as though Andy Hastings was a-runnin' away with her!" panted Beebee, wiping the dust and gravel out of his face.

"Looks t' me as though that team was runnin' away with both of 'em," grunted Sam Hall. "I felt sorry for her. I never done a dirty trick like that before, and if it hadn't been for yore wife —"

"Yore wife was as bad as mine, Sam."

"Worse. Old Hennery Goff won't speak to either one of us now, 'cause we out-voted him. Well, I hope them wimmin will be satisfied."

"Mine won't be," wailed Beebee. "She showed her stren'th. Next time she opens her mouth about the school, I'll resign. I'm jist as ashamed as you are, Sam — mebby more."

"Yo're pretty damn low in yore own estimation, if yuh are."

The killing of Shearer and robbery of the bank awoke Pineville to the realization that some very bad actors were in their midst, and as a result quite a crowd of men met at Hootie's store that night in sort of an indignation meeting.

Their criticism of the sheriff's office was rather more destructive than constructive, because none of them had any ideas worth working on. Mort Heffner was called in to give his opinion, and admitted that there was nothing his office could do.

"We hired a detective," he told them. "The cattle association sent us a man, who was warned out of the country, before he had a chance to do much. You men know how much chance a detective would have around here. The sheriff wants to stop these killings and robberies as much as you do, but he can't do a thing."

"Ain't nobody safe," complained Lester Cline.

"Not if they've got money," added Beebee.

"Well," declared Sam Hall angrily, "if the law don't do somethin' pretty soon, we'll take the law in our own hands."

Heffner laughed shortly. "You probably heard somebody say that, Sam. But go ahead and take the law in your own hands. It is your privilege to apprehend criminals. Don't let me stop you, gentlemen. In fact, I wish you would do something."

Hashknife and Sleepy were rather amused at the expressed opinions of those present, but left the meeting before it broke up and went to the Stormy River saloon, where they found old Luke Jones at the bar, telling the wide world that he had not been treated right by the TD outfit.

His prune whiskey jag had left him in a bitter frame of mind. His shirt and overalls were bespecked with hay from the livery stable, and one lock of his thin hair stuck straight out from his forehead, like an accusing finger.

"Fired because I sung," he declared. "Thasall I done; jist sung m'self out of a job."

"There's different grades of songs," said the bartender.

"Mine's top-hand," declared Luke. "I'm a natcheral singer. No sense in firin' a natcheral singer, is there? We're few and far between. And I'm a cook too. You ask Tolman. And you jist wait 'till he hears about me bein' fired by that squirt of a Shorty Gallup. Gimme liquor, that my gorge may not rise and suffy-cate me."

"You've been with the TD a long time, ain't yuh, Luke?"

"Long? My gosh! When I came here, Stormy River was jist a little spring."

Luke leered around, as though challenging anybody to dispute that statement. He fixed his eyes on Hashknife, and a smile twisted his lips.

"C'mere and have a drink. I 'member you, tall feller. You 'member me? I was the cook at the TD the mornin' Grimes quit out there. I shore 'member you. C'mon and have drink."

"I remember yuh," grinned Hashknife. He didn't want the drink, but he did want to get acquainted with Luke Jones.

"Invite yore pardner," said Luke. "Put out the glasses, bartender; we're havin' comp'ny. Say!" He turned to Hashknife. "I'm fired. They can all go to — , as far as I'm concerned. I jist had two good friends on that ranch. One was Buck Dennig and the other was Grimes. One's gone to a better land, and the other stayed around here."

"They tell me Buck Dennig was a fine feller," said Hashknife.

"You didn't know him? Pardner, he was a *man*."

"That's what I've heard."

"Beloved by everybody." Luke tried to keep back the tears.

"That's what I've heard. But they never found out who killed him."

"Never." Luke wiped the tears away with the back of his hand. "And they never will."

"Yuh think they won't," asked Hashnife softly. Luke was not too drunk. He looked sharply at Hashknife.

"What do you know?" he asked.

"Nothin'." Hashknife toyed with his glass. "But murder will always out, yuh know, Jones."

"Thasall right."

"What do you know, Jones?"

Luke paused with the glass at his lips. He placed it on the bar and squinted at himself in the mirror. "I don't know nothin' — much."

Some other men came in, and Luke shifted his interest to them. Hashknife knew there was nothing more to be learned from Luke Jones at present, but he had a feeling that the former TD cook knew something.

"Have yuh got anythin' to work on at all?" asked Sleepy, as they went to bed that night.

"Two murders and three robberies," smiled Hashknife. "And not to mention the fact that we're still here and our eight hours were up a long time ago."

"They were bluffin', Hashknife."

"Mebby."

"Well, they ain't made good."

"The note didn't say they'd kill us five minutes after our time was up. Give 'em time, cowboy."

CHAPTER TEN

Tex Blanco stopped short in the centre of the living room at the B Arrow and looked at Marion. Tex had been working late, and was still clad in his wide, bat-wing chaps, his features streaked with dust. He had left the ranch about the time Andy Hastings had gone to Pineville, and did not know Marion had come back with him.

"I didn't think you'd come," he said. "I told Andy I didn't think yuh would, but he said he'd try."

"I guess I just came," said Marion simply.

Tex shook his head slowly. "I — we all wanted yuh to come, Marion; but I think we did wrong in askin' yuh to come out here."

"It doesn't make any difference — now. You see, I've lost my school."

"You've lost yore school?" He came toward her. "I don't know what yuh mean, Marion."

She shrugged her shoulders wearily. "Just lost it. They hired a man to take my place."

"They hired a man — but why?"

"Oh, it doesn't matter. They said I wasn't satisfactory."

Tex stared at her for a moment.

"They know that wasn't true," he said firmly. "And you know it too, Marion. It was my fault. Oh, I know; it was because I came there. I'm to blame for you losin' that job."

Marion shook her head. "No, that wasn't it."

"Oh, I know. I — I guess I contaminated the kids."

He turned away and flung his sombrero on a chair.

"Jimmy told me what the children said. And they don't talk, unless they hear things at home. How is he, Marion?"

"Sleeping. The doctor promised to come out tonight. You heard what happened in Pineville?"

"Judd told me."

Mrs. Blanco came in from the kitchen, and Tex went to her, bending down to kiss the little old lady.

"Ye are a little late," she said. "But I've kept the supper warm. And were ye surprised to see the lady with us? Ah, it was fine of her to come. Do ye know it, the boy went fast asleep when she talked to him, Tex?"

"It was mighty fine of her to come," warmly. "Jimmy will get well now."

"He will, thanks to a most unselfish young lady. Ah, ye are unselfish, though."

Mrs. Blanco put her arms around Marion's waist, patting her on the arm.

"Do ye know, my dear, you are the first woman to come in this house in years?"

"I don't understand what you mean," smiled Marion.

"They'd know in Pineville. Folks avoid this place, as though it had a plague. 'Tis a bad reputation the B

Arrow has. Aye, that's a fact. They say that the old lady smokes a pipe. And she does. She may put unclean things in her mouth, but — but never mind. Tex, I'll set ye a supper."

She patted Marion on the arm and hurried away to get the supper for Tex.

"I think she's wonderful," said Marion.

Tex nodded slowly. "You don't know half of it, Marion. She's my silver linin'. I'd have left this country a long time ago, but for her. The Spanish half of me gets mad and wants to run away, but the Irish half listens to her — and I stay. What pleasure can she get out of life? No women ever come here. You don't know what it means to be shunned. When I take her to Pineville the women avoid her. They all avoid me too. But that doesn't hurt me.

"That's what a reputation will do, Marion. I've killed men in fair fights. They had an even break. But they call me a killer. I'm not a killer. God knows, I'm not. And then some dirty voiced liar hinted that we stole cattle. It don't take long for such things to get around. Killers and cow thieves! No wonder they leave us alone.

"They say I killed Buck Dennig." Tex laughed bitterly. He started to say something about the stage robbery, but checked himself in time. Mrs. Blanco called him from the kitchen, and he went out to her.

Marion sat down on a couch, covered with a gaudy blanket. It was quite cool, and one of the boys had built a fire in the big fireplace. The flames crackled merrily, and a little yellow canary in a home-made cage began singing softly.

Old Doctor Brent came before Tex finished supper. Jimmy was still asleep, and the doctor was well satisfied. Mrs. Blanco told him the effect Marion had had on Jimmy, and the old doctor thanked her for coming.

"I don't blame Jimmy." He smiled, looking closely at Marion, as they were introduced. "Don't blame him in the least. Fact of the matter is, I envy Jimmy."

He chuckled to himself, as he gave them orders. As he left he put a hand on Marion's shoulder.

"Mrs. Cooper told me about the school," he said. "Don't worry about it. I hope you can stay here until the boy is out of danger."

"Oh, I don't think I can stay here very long, doctor."

"I don't expect him to be sick very long."

That night the cowboys all sat around the living room, telling stories. Little Jimmy was worse, and babbled incessantly about the school. No one went to bed. The cowboys drowsed heavily, awoke to roll a cigarette, and drowsed some more. They were all fond of Jimmy.

Morning came. Jimmy went to sleep and the cowboys dragged out to breakfast. It was about nine o'clock when Mrs. Cooper came. It was the first time she had ever been on the ranch, but Mrs. Blanco greeted her warmly. Marion was asleep on a couch in the living room, but awoke at sound of Mrs. Cooper's voice.

Ma Cooper fairly hugged her.

"I met Mrs. Beebee this mornin'," chuckled Ma Cooper. "She tried to avoid me, but I cornered her, and what I told her would take the polish off a mahogany table. Whoo-ee-e-e! Oh, we had it hot and heavy. She swears you eloped with Andy Hastings. Ha, ha, ha, ha! Well, how's the little boy?"

"He's asleep, Ma Cooper. Had a bad night, though. The doctor wants me to stay here until Jimmy is better."

Mrs. Cooper lifted her brows quickly, a smile in her eyes.

"The doctor does, eh? Well, always obey the doctor, Honey."

Marion flushed quickly, as she added: —

"But I can't very well do that, Ma Cooper."

"Why not? Bless your heart, of course yuh can — if yuh want to. I'll send yore trunk out. And when yuh get all through with the *doctor's* orders, come back and live with us. Hootie says he misses yuh. That's quite an honor. He never misses me."

The three women sat down and talked for an hour. Mrs. Blanco seemed to grow younger every minute. Tex came in and stood against the dining room entrance, listening to the chatter, a smile on his lips.

He tiptoed through the hall and went to the bedroom, where Andy was sitting beside the bed. Little Jimmy was awake, but his little face looked pinched and drawn, and his blue eyes clouded. He knew Tex, and smiled.

"Hallo, little pardner," said Tex softly.

"He asked for yuh, Tex," said Andy. "Asked me to have yuh sing to him."

"Sing to him? Jimmy, do yuh want me to sing to yuh?"

"About the rose, Uncle Tex," weakly.

Tex looked queerly at Andy. A strange request for a sick boy. But Tex turned to a corner and picked up an old guitar, which he had not played for a long time. Softly he tuned it, while the little fellow watched him wearily.

He began singing softly in a crooning tenor, and little Jimmy closed his eyes, listening. Andy rested his chin on his hands, tears in his eyes. Out in the living room the three women stopped talking and listened.

"He's singing to the lad," whispered Mrs. Blanco. "It's the song he likes best. Listen —"

"You may search everywhere, but none can compare with my wild Irish Rose."

"He calls it his rose song."

". . . And some day for my sake, they may let me take the bloom from my wild Irish Rose."

The voice crooned the end of the song. Ma Cooper held out her hand to Mrs. Blanco.

"I'm goin' now," she said softly. "I'm glad I heard the song, Mrs. Blanco — and I'll come again. When yuh come to Pineville, come and see me, will yuh? Marion, I'll send out yore trunk."

She hurried out to the buckboard and rode away, leaving Marion and Mrs. Blanco in the doorway, looking after her.

"That song made her cry," said Mrs. Blanco softly.

"It almost made me cry too," confessed Marion.

Tex came out, closing the door softly behind him.

"He's asleep again," said Tex. "He was awake and knew me and Andy. Can yuh imagine it; he asked me to sing."

"I — I don't blame him," said Marion. "We heard you."

"Pshaw! I was just singin' for Jimmy."

Ma Cooper sent the team spinning over the road to Pineville. She was glad she had visited the B Arrow, and she decided to go again. As strange as it may seem, she had never exchanged a dozen words with Mrs. Blanco before — and she had found her a delightful old Irish lady.

"Got a lot more class than some of these Pineville holier-than-thous," she declared to herself. "And everybody said she was an ignorant old pipe smoker! Ignorant! If some of 'em had half her brains they'd die from headache."

She drove up in front of Hootie's store and found Oscar Johnson, who seemed to have nothing better to do than to brace up one of the porch posts.

"Are yuh awful busy, Oscar?" she asked.

"Not right now, Mrs. Cooper."

"I was just wonderin' if you'd do me a big favor."

"Wouldn't be a bit surprised." He grinned.

"Well, I've got to get somebody to take this team and haul Miss Evans' truck out to the B Arrow Ranch."

"Out to the B Arrow Ranch? Oh, yeah — shore. Is she goin' to stay out there?"

"Long enough to need her trunk."

"Uh-huh. Want me to go right away, Mrs. Cooper?"

"If you'll do it, Oscar."

"Ain't a bit busy."

"Well, get in and we'll load up at the house."

Oscar carried the trunk down to the buckboard. The back of the vehicle was hardly large enough to accommodate the trunk, and Oscar had no ropes to tie it on.

"But I reckon it'll ride there," he told her, as he climbed in. "I'll take it easy."

He drove out of town, holding the team in check. The last time he had driven a buggy team he had smashed the buggy, and he was going to be more careful this time. Everything went well, until the crossing of Stormy River, and he swung a little too far down the stream, where some big boulders blocked a wheel and almost upset the buckboard, and threw the trunk into the river.

Oscar yelled like a Comanche, whipped the team to the shore, where he tied them to a snag, and then went galloping down the stream after the trunk, which had wedged on a sand bar, twenty feet below where it went into the water.

"My God, if I ever do anythin' right, I'll die next minute," declared Oscar, sloshing out of the river with the trunk in his arms, with the water running a stream from one of the corners.

He placed the trunk on the sand and surveyed it sadly.

"Wetter 'n hell!"

He sat down on it, removed his boots and poured out the water, while the team watched him; possibly wondering what it was all about. It suddenly occurred to him that he might be able to dry out things; so he opened the trunk, which was not locked.

It was fairly well filled with feminine attire, the top things being dry. He dumped them out on the sand, grunting disgustedly when he found the things sodden in the bottom of the trunk.

"Well, f'r gosh sake!" he grunted, and lifted a big, pearl-handled Colt .45 from the bottom of the trunk. It was fully loaded.

Ignoring the rest of the things, Oscar sat down, with his back against the trunk and examined the gun. Oscar was not very quick minded, but something seemed to tell him that a school teacher, under ordinary conditions, would not own a new gun of that size and description.

He removed the cartridges and amused himself for a while by snapping it at different objects. He liked the trigger pull, and the balance of the weapon. The pearl flashed in the sun like an opal, as Oscar polished it with a none too clean handkerchief.

He took out his own gun and compared them. They were the same model, same calibre. But Oscar's gun was shiny in spots, nicked, the trigger pull altogether too heavy for accurate work. In fact, Oscar's gun was old. Suddenly a bright idea occurred to Oscar.

He took his pocket knife and unscrewed the handles of both guns and changed handles, putting the pearl ones on his own gun. Now he had a new gun with old handles, while his old gun, resplendent in mother of pearl, went into the bottom of the trunk, along with the sodden clothes.

"What would a school ma'am want of a new gun, anyway?" he asked himself. "A gun's a gun. It ain't stealin', if yuh put back as good as yuh take."

Thereupon, Oscar loaded the things back in the trunk, put it back on the buckboard and headed for the B Arrow. Marion was asleep, much to Oscar's relief, and Mrs. Blanco told him to leave the trunk on the porch. Oscar left it in a sunny place, hoping to dry it out a little, at least.

He drove back, stabled the horses in Cooper's barn, and went back to the office well satisfied with himself. The inquest over the body of Guy Shearer was held that afternoon. Hashknife and Sleepy attended, but were not called as witnesses. The usual verdict was rendered by the jury.

The sheriff had heard a number of remarks reflecting on his ability as a peace officer, and he was not in a good frame of mind when he went back to his office with Oscar.

"What do they expect me to do?" he asked plaintively. "I never had no trainin' at this here job. My God, to hear some of them whipoorwills talkin', you'd think I ought to have an X-ray eye. I'm sick of the whole danged job."

"Same here," agreed Oscar. "I took this job to help you out, Pat — and you don't need no help, not for what you've done."

"We're a awful mess, Oscar."

"Speak for yourself — I'm all right for what I'm intended. A deputy ain't supposed to have any brains."

Oscar took off his heavy belt and gun and placed them on the desk, after which he sighed deeply and stretched out on a cot. The sheriff stared sad-eyed at the belt and gun, thinking over the woes of his position.

His fingers picked absently at the cartridges in the belt loops.

He ran his fingers over the butt of the gun, not because he wanted to feel the gun, but because of something to do. Then he shut one eye and looked at the exposed breech of the gun. After a moment's scrutiny he drew the gun from the holster and looked at it closely.

"Where'd yuh git the new gun, Oscar?" he asked.

Oscar sat up like a mechanical toy — quick and jerky.

"Wh-what gun?"

"This here one." The sheriff held it up.

"Oh, that one."

Oscar swore inwardly at himself for leaving that gun on the desk.

"New gun, ain't it, Oscar?"

"Pretty new." Oscar sank down again.

"Pretty damn new, it looks to me. You never had it before."

"No," said Oscar. "It's almost new, Pat."

"Where'd yuh get it?"

"Where'd I get it?"

"Yeah; where'd yuh get it?"

"Oh, I dunno."

"Yuh dunno?"

"Well, my God!" Oscar sat up and glowered at the sheriff. "What's the difference where I got it? When you start harpin' on anything', yuh never know when to quit."

"I ain't harpin'. I just asked yuh where yuh got it."

"Where I got it, eh? Ain't that harpin'?"

"Well, I just asked yuh. Yo're my deputy. Ain't I got a right to ask yuh where yuh got a new gun?"

"Got a right — yes."

"Well, where didja get it, Oscar?"

"Yuh mean — who did I get it *from?*"

"If that's the answer — yes."

"I didn't get it from nobody."

"Didja find it?"

Oscar got off the cot and hitched up his pants. He was mad enough to tell where and how he got it — and he did. The sheriff listened, open mouthed, while Oscar described how he lost the school teacher's trunk in Stormy River, how he recovered it and wanted to dry out the clothes, and where he found the new gun.

"And that answers yore question, Pat," he finished. "Now forgit it, will yuh?"

"And you took the pearl handles off it and put 'em on yore old smoke wagon, eh? Yuh traded guns — Oscar Johnson, you — fool!" The sheriff got to his feet and advanced on the cot, half-choking as he tried to talk.

"O-o-oh, you blame fool!" he wailed. "Who had a new six-gun with pearl handles? Who did? Tex Blanco! He lost it at that hold-up. That's what them wimmin stopped and picked up. That teacher got it. She's stuck on Tex, Oscar. She put the gun in her trunk, and you — you traded — oh, my God! Oscar you've ruined the evidence!"

Oscar sat up, rubbing his nose. Then he got to his feet and hitched up his pants. He looked at the sheriff sadly and shook his head.

"Well, dang yuh, yuh kept on harpin' until yuh got an answer, didn't yuh. Curiosity killed the cat — and it made you pretty damn sick. Now, what'll we do?"

"Keep our mouths shut!" snapped the sheriff. "If we ever let this get out, they'll laugh us out of the valley."

"Well, I'm not goin' to tell it. My gosh, didn't I try to even keep it from you?"

"You jist the same as stole that gun."

"I traded," said Oscar firmly. "Mine had a heavy pull on the trigger, and it throwed me off. Some day I might accidentally kill somebody."

The sheriff stumped around the office, while Oscar lay down again and began rolling a cigarette. Finally the sheriff sat down again, holding his head in his hands.

"If I had knowed about that gun," said Oscar slowly. "But I never once thought about the school ma'am havin' Tex's gun in her trunk. Why should I? I never even remembered that Tex had a pearl handle six-gun. I remember it now."

"It's too late now. It's an old gun that's got the pearl handles on it now. Tex could laugh at us."

"Unless yuh might make that girl admit findin' it, Pat. If yuh caught her before she found that gun in the trunk. Even at that she might not see that the gun was different."

"Yuh mean we might bluff her into admittin' that her and Mrs. Cooper found the gun there?"

"Why not? If we could get the gun, without Tex seein' it, we can change the handles back again."

"Yeah, we might do that."

The sheriff sighed and lifted his head. It was worth a try. He started to suggest something more, but stopped short. Hashknife Hartley was standing in the doorway, leaning against the door frame, slowly rolling a cigarette, his face very grave.

"We might bluff her," said Oscar. "But she's got to be talked to before she empties that trunk, Pat. She'll see it's been tampered with, and she'll get scared and give Tex back his gun."

Hashknife looked at Oscar, who was lying on his back, staring at the ceiling, all oblivious to Hashknife's presence. The sheriff cleared his throat harshly, glared at Oscar murderously.

"It won't be any job to change the handles," said Oscar.

"Are you goin' to keep runnin' off at the mouth?" asked the sheriff explosively.

Oscar sat up, took one look at Hashknife and sank back.

"He's got the hoof-and-mouth disease," said the sheriff wearily. "Every time he opens his mouth he gets his foot in it."

"The inquest didn't amount to much," said Hashknife.

"Not much. How could it?"

"Did Shearer have any relatives, Sheriff?"

"In Chicago, I think. Rice sent some telegrams, and we'll wait to hear what they want done with the body."

"None around here, eh?"

"Matt Sturgis is a forty-second cousin, or somethin' like that."

"Sturgis of the TD outfit?"

"Yeah. Shearer worked over at Garnet quite a while. Nice sort of a feller."

"What kind of a person was Buck Dennig?"

"Wild as a hawk, but square as a die."

"Get along well with Tolman?"

"Oh, shore."

"Like hell!" snorted Oscar. "They used to quarrel a lot. Yuh must remember I worked for 'em."

"Quarrel over what?" asked the sheriff. "I never heard it."

"Over money. Cleve Tolman gambled on the stock markets, and he got stuck a couple times pretty hard. Buck was a gambler too, but not on the markets. I heard 'em hot and heavy one night a year or so ago. I reckon Cleve had used some of the partnership money. Anyway, they decided to each bank their share after that."

"I found out after Buck's death that they had separate bank accounts," said the sheriff. "But I never knowed why."

"Well, that was why," said Oscar. "Buck shore was mad, and he gave Tolman hell. I couldn't help hearin' it. I thought it was all off with the partnership, but next day they was all right again. But outside of their quarrels, they was good enough friends, I reckon."

Hashknife left the office in a few minutes. He had heard enough to know that in some way Oscar Johnson had found the gun in Marion's trunk, and had left his gun in its place. And he had also heard enough to know that the sheriff intended getting a confession, if possible, and recovering the evidence.

But both the sheriff and deputy were afraid that Hashknife had heard too much.

"I don't sabe that feller," declared Oscar. "Yuh don't know whether he's for yuh or against yuh."

"Well," said the sheriff sadly, "he prob'ly knows that it ain't Tex's gun in that trunk. He kinda antagonizes me."

"Yuh don't suppose he's in cahoots with Tex, do yuh?"

"You git some real bright ideas, Oscar. Nossir, Tex Blanco held up that stage, as sure as shootin'. Mebby him and Judd. Anyway, there was more than one man. We won't do nothin' now, Oscar. We'll wait until dark, and then go out to the B Arrow. We've got to take a chance that she ain't found that gun. And even if she has, she wouldn't rec'nise it."

"That's a good idea," applauded Oscar. "But I hope Tex ain't there. Anyway, he don't know about that gun; so we're safe, as far as that's concerned."

Hashknife found Sleepy at the Stormy River bar, talking with Frank Shell, the owner of the saloon, and Dobe Severn. Matt Sturgis, Shorty Gallup and Alex McLean were playing pool at the rear of the room.

"What became of old Luke Jones?" asked Hashknife.

"He went to Garnet this mornin'," said Dobe. "Sobered up and pulled out, I guess. He'll probably get drunk in Garnet. He shore raised hell at the TD. Got drunk on prune whisky and pot-shotted everythin' around the place."

Hashknife wanted a chance to talk seriously with the old cook. Luke Jones had admitted that he knew something, and Hashknife wanted to know what that something might be. Sleepy went with him from the saloon, and they crossed the street to the bank, which was closed. Hashknife knew where John Rice lived, and they found the old banker at home.

"I'll tell yuh what I want to see," explained Hashknife. "Buck Dennig cashed a cheque for ten thousand dollars the afternoon of the night he was killed, and I want to see that cancelled cheque, if it still exists."

"Why, I suppose it still exists," said Rice. "But what is the idea of *you* wanting to see it?"

"Curiosity, I reckon, Mr. Rice."

"I'm sorry, but I —"

"Do you think Buck Dennig committed suicide?"

"That would have been impossible, Hartley."

"And yuh don't think he buried that ten thousand before he died, do yuh?"

"Buried it? Why would he bury it?"

"All right; he was murdered and robbed. If it isn't too much trouble, I'd like to see that cheque."

The old banker's mild blue eyes wavered under the steady stare of the gray ones, and he turned slowly on his heel.

"Wait until I get my hat," he said. "I — I suppose there would be no harm in it, Hartley."

They walked back to the bank, where Rice unlocked it, and they went inside. It did not take Rice long to find the cheque, along with Buck Dennig's statement and several other smaller cheques, drawn by Buck. Hashknife spread them all out on the counter and examined them closely. He was not an expert on handwriting, but his eyes were keen. Finally he took out the warning note he had received, and examined it again.

The old banker did not seem interested. The cancelled cheques meant nothing to Sleepy, who talked with Rice about the murder and robbery. It seemed that there was a difference in the opinions of the several directors of the bank, and no final decision had been made as to how soon the bank would resume operations.

"I suppose Cleve Tolman has taken over the TD Ranch, ain't he?" asked Hashknife.

"Yes," nodded the banker. "I believe he has a court order to that effect. Buck Dennig died intestate, and as far as any one knows, he has no relatives. Naturally, the ranch and all of Dennig's personal goods belong to Tolman."

Hashknife folded up the statement and cheques, handing them back to Rice.

"Thank yuh, Mr. Rice," he said. "Keep those where we can get at 'em, in case we need 'em again."

"Yes, certainly. Are you a — a detective, Mr. Hartley?"

"Under the circumstances," smiled Hashknife.

"What was the queer idea of lookin' at them cheques?" asked Sleepy, after they left the bank.

"Just playin' a hunch, Sleepy. After supper we're ridin' to Garnet to have a talk with Luke Jones. I hope he's sober enough to come clean, or drunk enough to talk."

"Have yuh hit the trail, cowboy?"

"I dunno. Anyway, I've got a couple blazes in sight."

CHAPTER ELEVEN

Marion did not discover that her trunk had been soaked in the river. Mrs. Blanco had ordered one of the cowboys to move it into the room Marion was occupying, and she had had no cause to open it. Little Jimmy was so sick that both women spent most of their time in the room with him.

Tex came in from work about five o'clock. The doctor had not been there since morning; so Tex sent Corbett after him. Tex was pleased to find that Marion's trunk had been brought to the ranch. Neither Tex nor Marion had mentioned that gun again, and Tex did not know that Marion suspected Hashknife of overhearing what she had told Tex that night about finding his gun at the scene of the hold-up.

Tex had offered no explanation, no alibi. Marion did not want to believe that Tex robbed that stage, but the evidence was all against him.

The doctor did not get there until after supper, and decided to stay a while and watch the patient. Mrs. Blanco sat in the bedroom with the doctor and Andy Hastings, while Tex and Marion sat in front of the fireplace in the living room.

"It's funny how things break," said Tex. "Who would ever have bet on any kind of odds that you would ever be stayin' here at the B Arrow, Marion?"

"I suppose not."

"But I'm glad yuh are. I'm sorry for little Jimmy, but his sickness brought me luck. It gave me a chance to see yuh for more than a minute at a time."

Marion stared in the flames, her chin resting on one palm.

"I know what yo're thinkin'," he said slowly. "I'm no fool. Yo're thinkin' how much better it would be if I was a respectable citizen, instead of a man under suspicion of bein' a murderer, stage robber and a lot of other crimes."

"I wasn't thinking of that, Tex," quickly.

"But I am, yuh know."

"I don't *know* it, Tex."

They sat there together for a long time, saying nothing, while the flames crackled in the old fireplace. Finally Tex walked over to a table, picked up an old photograph album and brought it over to Marion.

"Some of the old Blanco family," he said, opening the old book. "Oh, they were respectable enough, I suppose. I'm the black sheep of the family. Some of those tin-types are rather good. There's my father, when he was twenty. I reckon he was a gay young blade of Seville.

"Always wanted to be a bull fighter, he said. Came to California to pick up gold on the streets."

Tex laughed shortly. "Didn't find the gold; so he went into the cattle business — and found it. That next one is an uncle of mine. He was a bull fighter in Mexico City, until he found a bull that was color blind. Saw the man instead of the red cloth."

Mrs. Blanco came from the bedroom.

"The doctor is still there," she said. "He thinks the lad is gettin' along well."

"I was just showing Marion some old pictures," said Tex smiling.

"Aye — and they're old, too," smiled Mrs. Blanco.

Some kodak pictures had been left between the leaves of the album, and as Tex started to gather them up, Marion stopped him, and took one of the pictures. It was a very good snap-shot of Tex and another man, standing close together, holding their big hats in their hands, with a corner of a corral fence for a background. The faces were well lighted.

Marion stared at the picture for several moments, and her face was white as she looked up at Tex.

"Who is that — that man with you, Tex?" she asked.

"That?" Tex laughed shortly. "That's Buck Dennig."

"Buck Dennig? The man who was — who was killed?"

"Yes, Marion," softly. "Go ahead and say it."

"Buck Dennig."

"It was taken about five years ago, Marion."

"Did you know anything about him, Tex?"

"Why, what's the matter?" asked Mrs. Blanco. "Your face is all white, lass."

Marion shook her head, and her hands trembled, as she examined the picture again, staring down at the smiling face of Buck Dennig.

"Nobody knew much about him," said Tex. "He had no relatives, I guess. He never spoke about his past. I don't —"

Came a sharp knock on the front door. Tex walked over and opened the door, admitting the sheriff and deputy. They did not stop to wait for an invitation to enter. Oscar stopped at the doorway, while the sheriff advanced toward Marion and Mrs. Blanco. Tex still had his hand on the door.

"I've been talkin' to Mrs. Cooper," said the sheriff, addressing Marion. "She didn't want to get in bad with the law, so she talked quite a lot. Now, it's yore turn. I want that pearl-handled six shooter you've got in yore trunk."

Marion's face was whiter now, as she looked up at the grim-faced sheriff, her mind trying to conceive that Ma Cooper had divulged their secret.

"What pearl-handled six shooter are you talkin' about?" demanded Tex.

The sheriff did not turn his head, as he replied:

"That's my business with this young lady; you keep out of it."

"That's what I say," growled Oscar, trying to keep his nerve.

"Mrs. Cooper told you?" Marion's voice was a whisper.

"Shore thing. Now, you dig up that gun. I could put yuh in jail for doin' a thing like that. Hurry up."

"What did she tell you?" asked Marion weakly.

"About you findin' that gun at the hold-up. We know whose gun it is, and we're goin' —"

Tex acted quickly. In fact, he acted so quickly that Oscar Johnson's feet went from under him and he fell along the wall, clawing for support, his holster dangling empty, and when the sheriff turned Oscar crashed down on the floor, and they heard the porch railing creak as Tex vaulted it.

The sheriff sprang toward the doorway, while Oscar swore bitterly and got back to his feet, feeling for his gun, which Tex had taken away.

"Let him go!" snapped the sheriff. "We'll get him, Oscar. What we want right now is that six-gun. Where's the trunk?"

But before Marion could tell him, from somewhere out in the darkness came the thudding report of a revolver shot. In another moment came a spatter of shots, as though several guns were discharged close together. A space of possibly five seconds, and three more shots, spaced about two seconds apart.

The sheriff and deputy seemed rooted to the spot, unable to understand what it was all about. Outside somebody was shouting questions, a man swore wonderingly. Frank Judd ran up the steps to the front door and stepped inside, staring at the sheriff and deputy.

"What in hell is goin' on around here?" he demanded.

"God knows, I don't," said the sheriff.

Some one came into the kitchen, and they all went into the dining room. It was Hashknife Hartley, half-carrying, half-dragging Sleepy Stevens. Hashknife's face was white in the lamp light. The doctor had stepped out from the bedroom, and now he went straight to Hashknife.

"In here," said Mrs. Blanco. "On the couch. Don't lay him on the floor."

Judd grasped Sleepy's feet, and they carried him in to the living room couch.

"For gosh sake, what happened?" asked the sheriff. He had forgotten all about the trunk.

Hashknife shook his head, his lips shut tightly, while the doctor cut away Sleepy's vest and shirt, trying to determine the extent of his injuries. So interested were they that they did not see Tex Blanco return.

Marion was first to see him. He was standing in the doorway, leaning weakly against the wall, while the left shoulder of his pale-blue silk shirt was gradually assuming a scarlet cast. The blood seemed to have drained from his face, and his brown eyes were filled with pain.

"Tex!" whispered Marion. "Oh, Tex; you're hurt!"

"It's all right," he said weakly. "I'm all right."

Hashknife stepped over and helped Tex to a chair, where he slumped wearily. Hashknife tore away the shirt and began mopping away the blood. Tex had been shot rather high up through the shoulder, and from the way he carried his arm Hashknife felt sure that no bones were broken.

"In the name of God, what happened?" demanded the sheriff. "Who done all the shootin', anyway, Hartley?"

Hashknife shook his head, and watched the doctor.

"Nasty wound," said the doctor. "Rib probably saved his life. Broke the rib, but turned the bullet. Went all the way through, but turned aside enough to give him a mighty good chance. Mrs. Blanco, will you get me plenty of hot water and cloths?"

He got up from the floor and walked over to Tex, who was gritting his teeth to keep upright.

"Lucky all around," muttered the doctor. "Clean through and never touched the bone. Miss Evans, you can help me, if you will."

He had noticed that Marion was on the verge of keeling over in a faint; so he used these means of bracing her nerve. "Go out and help Mrs. Blanco fix the water. Nobody is going to die, my dear. Regular hospital we've got here. Sheriff, if you can't think of anything else to do, try closing your mouth. It has been open for five minutes."

"Well, bub-by Gawd!" snorted the sheriff. "Won't nobody tell me what happened? Two wounded men, and no explanation."

"I don't know, Sheriff," said Hashknife, looking down at Sleepy. "We rode in here — down by the gate — and somebody shot Sleepy. I didn't know he was hit until he fell off near the back door out there. I was shootin' at the flashes."

"I shot at somebody," muttered Tex. "But they shot me first. There was a lot of shootin', I think."

"Plenty," said Hashknife grimly.

"Why did you come out here, Hartley?" asked the sheriff.

"Why did you come out here?" retorted Hashknife.

"I guess you knew why. I came out here to get that gun, and I'm goin' to get it. You keep yore nose out of my business, will yuh? I've got the goods on Tex Blanco, and I'll put that girl in jail with him for tryin' to destroy evidence. I don't know what yore game is, but you better not monkey with the law."

"I'm not monkeyin' with the law," said Hashknife. He looked at Frank Judd, who had been shifting around nervously. "Go and get Miss Evans' trunk and bring it here, Judd."

"You never mind!" snapped the sheriff. "I'll get that there trunk and —"

"Aw, quit bluffin'," said Hashknife. "Get the trunk, Judd."

Judd brought the trunk and placed it in the centre of the room.

"Open it up and find a six shooter in it, will yuh?" requested Hashknife. The sheriff swore impotently, as Judd dug deeply in the trunk. Mrs. Blanco and Marion came in, bringing the hot water and cloths, and Marion stopped short at the sight of Frank Judd, digging in her trunk. Finally he straightened up, holding the pearlhandled gun in his hand.

Hashknife took it from him and showed it to Marion.

"Is that the gun you found at the place of the hold up?"

"Yes," she whispered.

"Fine," smiled Hashknife. He walked over to Tex and held it before him.

"Is that yore gun, Tex?" he asked. Tex stared at it for a moment, looked up at Hashknife blankly.

"That's not my gun," he said evenly. "My gun was new."

"That's what I thought," said Hashknife seriously. He turned the gun over in his hands, looking at it closely.

"There's two initials scratched on the bottom of the trigger guard," he said slowly. "Looks like O.J."

Hashknife looked keenly at Oscar Johnson, but the deputy was not interested enough to look at him. Hashknife stepped over and handed the gun to the sheriff.

"There's yore evidence, Sheriff," smiling.

The sheriff's face was a study in mixed emotions. He knew that the evidence was ruined now. His idea was to have secured the gun, switched the handles again, and swear the new gun was the one found in the trunk. He looked at Oscar, and longed to bend the gun over his thick head. But all he could do was to accept defeat gracefully.

"All right, Hartley," he said thickly. "You'll hear more of this later. I'm not through with you — yet."

"Well, that's fine, Sheriff."

Oscar followed the sheriff away from the ranch, glad to be out of the house, while Hashknife and Judd helped the doctor. Sleepy was still unconscious when they put him to bed. Hashknife wanted to take him to town, but the doctor would not listen to him.

"Right here he stays, Hartley, and right here I stay."

Tex refused to go to bed, but stretched out on the couch. He had lost considerable blood and the heavy bullet had shocked him badly, but he felt better now.

There were too many things to talk about for him to think of going to sleep.

He wanted to know how Oscar Johnson's revolver happened to be in Marion's trunk, and listened in amazement to what Hashknife told him. Of course, Hashknife did not hear all the story, but he had heard the sheriff and deputy say enough for him to build up the rest of the story.

"And you knew they would come after that gun tonight?" asked Marion.

"Wasn't sure; but I knew they intended to come and get it. They didn't want Tex to see that gun, until after they had switched handles again."

"You saved my bacon, Hartley," said Tex wearily. "They've got the goods on me, I guess. But I want you to know that I'm mighty grateful for what you've done for me."

"How grateful, Blanco?"

"I don't know what yuh mean, Hartley."

"Grateful enough to tell me about that hold-up?"

"To tell you what about it?"

"How yore pearl-handled gun happened to be there."

"Looks as though I lost it, don't it?"

"Let's stop sparrin' around, Blanco. Where was you when that stage was robbed?"

Tex turned his head and stared at the fire several minutes, while they waited for him to speak. Then:

"I didn't try to prove any alibi," he said slowly. "I'm not a good liar, and this sounds like a lie. Nobody would believe it, so I kept still. The night before the hold-up I was goin' to Garnet to the dance.

"I left the house and went down to the stable to get my horse. As I stepped into the stable, somethin' hit me on the head, and I didn't know anythin' for quite a while. When I woke up I was tied tight, gagged and blindfolded. I had an awful headache and a thirst. You've read about men gettin' loose from ropes? Well, I couldn't. I reckon I rubbed all the skin off my wrists.

"I don't know how long it was before somebody came. I knew it was daylight, because I had felt the sun for a long time. They unfastened my legs and helped me to my feet, but didn't say a word. It was hard for me to stand up, even when I braced my legs.

"Then a man spoke to me, and said he was goin' to cut my hands loose. He told me to leave the bandage on my eyes until I could count a hundred, before I took it off. He warned me that he was counting too, and if I took it off too quick, he'd kill me. Then he cut my hands loose.

"My gun was gone. I felt for it first. And I counted a hundred before I took off that blindfold and gag. Then I found myself in a little clearing in the brush, about two miles from here. My horse was there, tied to a snag. My head was so sore I had to wear my hat on one side of my head, and I was so thirsty I couldn't talk. So I came home. I told mother, because she would believe."

"Sounds reasonable," said Hashknife seriously.

"Don't say that," replied Tex. "It sounds like a badly told lie."

"And somebody stole your gun, trying to make them think you robbed the stage!" exclaimed Marion.

"If you believe my story," sighed Tex. "I can't hardly believe it myself."

"Oh, I'm glad I found that gun. Suppose the sheriff had found it, Tex."

"I'd be in jail, I suppose. But, Marion, just before the sheriff came in to-night, you were looking at Buck Dennig's picture. What was it all about?"

Marion went to her trunk, and after a few moments she came back and handed Tex a picture of a man.

"Why, that's Buck!" he said. "Buck Dennig."

"My brother," said Marion softly. "Blaine Evans."

"It's Buck Dennig all right," said Judd. "Little younger, but it's Buck, just the same, Miss Evans."

"Then Buck Dennig was my brother."

The doctor examined the picture, nodding slowly.

"That is the man we knew as Buck Dennig, Miss Evans."

"That's somethin' to shock Cleve Tolman," grinned Judd.

"They say I killed Buck Dennig," said Tex bitterly. "And I haven't even a good lie to use as an alibi. We quarrelled that night. I reckon I would have killed him, because he called me a thief."

"I don't believe you killed him," said Marion.

"Well, I can't prove it, Marion. I suppose they are sayin' that I killed Guy Shearer and robbed the bank."

Hashknife reached in his pocket and drew out the hondoo, which bore the brand of the B Arrow, and held it down in front of Tex.

"Who owns that hondoo, Tex?" he asked. Tex stared at it for a moment and took it in his good hand.

"That's mine," he said. "Where did you get it, Hartley?"

"On the floor of the bank, when we found Shearer. The rope was there too, but the hondoo had been cut off."

Tex stared at the hondoo, turning it over in his hand.

"You found that on the floor — my rope and hondoo?"

"The sheriff has the rope, I reckon. Yuh can't identify a rope."

"Does he know you've got this hondoo?"

"Nope. I sneaked it off the floor."

Tex lay back on his pillow and closed his eyes wearily.

"And I've got no lie to tell about that," he said. "I don't know who nor what you are, Hartley — but you've sure been a friend to me. That evidence would hang me."

"I suppose it would. Did you lose the rope?"

"I don't know. Never missed it, if I did."

"Any of yore boys carry a marked hondoo?"

"I don't think so. Do you know any, Frank?"

Judd shook his head quickly. "I guess not, Tex."

Hashknife put the hondoo on the mantel. "I'm goin' to Garnet," he told them. "Take good care of Sleepy, will yuh? He means more to me than anythin' on earth. I don't like to run away, when he's bogged down thataway, but he knows me and he'll understand why I went."

And without another word he went out to his horse and mounted in the dark.

"We better get you into a bed, Tex," suggested the doctor. "You probably don't realize that you are badly hurt."

"Yeah, I realize it, doc," said Tex. "But I'm all right, except that I don't know what it is all about. Who shot Stevens and me, I wonder? What was it all about, anyway?"

"I wish I knew," said Judd. "Andy is asleep in the bunk-house, and Tommy and Kit are in Pineville. I ran out of the bunk-house when the shootin' started, but I couldn't see anybody. Who would want to shoot 'em, Tex?"

"Search me. I think the sheriff was mad enough to shoot somebody; but he's no bushwhacker. Who are these two men, I wonder? Nobody seems to know much about 'em."

"They seem all right," said Marion softly.

"They *are* all right," declared Tex. "They've proved it to me. How badly is Stevens hurt, doc?"

"Bad enough to lay him up for a while."

The doctor went back to where Sleepy was lying. Little Jimmy had decided to sleep through it all, and the doctor was satisfied with his condition.

It was nearly midnight when Hashknife reached Garnet. He tied his horse at a hitch-rack near the Overland Saloon, the big gambling house of the town, and went in. The place was fairly well filled, and a number of games were running full blast.

Hashknife went along to the bar, where he stopped and looked over the room, which was hazy with tobacco smoke. He wanted to find Luke Jones, and he expected to find the hard-boiled old TD cook where the drinks came fast.

The room buzzed with conversation, the click of chips, the droning voices of the dealers, while glasses clicked at the bar and spurs rasped along the metal bar rail.

No one paid any attention to the tall cowboy, who leaned against the bar, smoking a cigarette. At the rear of the room were a number of tables, where drinks were served. The three-piece orchestra struck up a dance, and several of the chap-clad gentry tramped around the small dance space with the "girls," having a boisterous time.

Suddenly a girl screamed, and her scream was punctuated by the thudding jar of a revolver shot. The room was in an uproar in a moment. The girls scattered like a bevy of frightened quail. Hashknife shoved his way through the crowd, and found himself against a table, which had been upset by some one who stood not upon their manner of going.

A man was lying flat on his back on the floor, and against the wall, standing alone, gun in hand, was Cleve Tolman, owner of the TD outfit. Some men were moving in closer to him and he eyed them with evident hostility.

"Keep away from me," warned Tolman. "I shot in self-defense, that's all."

"That's right," said a cowboy, who had evidently seen the shooting. "The other feller went for his gun."

"Thank yuh," said Tolman coldly. He looked around and saw Hashknife, looking at him across the table.

"Somebody ought to get a doctor for him," he said, and several men left the saloon. Tolman slowly replaced the gun in his holster.

Hashknife stepped in close and looked at the man on the floor. It was old Luke Jones, ex-cook of the TD. Another man knelt down and lifted the old man's head and shoulders. But old Luke wasn't dead. He groaned a couple of times and opened his eyes.

It seemed as though he had some difficulty in realizing what had happened.

"Been drinkin' quite a lot," said one of the men. Luke looked at him, but shifted his eyes to Hashknife.

"Where's Tolman?" he asked hoarsely. "Didn't I git him?"

"I guess yuh didn't," said Hashknife. "Never mind; just take it easy, old timer; the doctor will get here in a few minutes."

"Aw, to hell with the doctor! I've got mine, I guess. So he beat me to it, eh? First time that's ever happened too. He wouldn't pay me to keep my mouth shut, Tolman wouldn't. All I wanted was a thousand dollars. That ain't much."

He blinked around at the faces, and added: "To keep yore mouth shut."

"Shut about what?" asked Hashknife softly.

"About Buck Dennig. I told him to give me the money, or I'll talk. He called me a dirty black somethin', and I went for my gun. Where is he, the dirty side-winder? Buck was my friend. I knowed more about Buck than anybody. Buck's got relatives. He's got a mother and a sister. Tolman didn't know it until to-night. He called me a damn liar, and then killed me to keep me from tellin' it."

"You ain't dead yet," said one of the men.

"No, but I'm darn close to it. And this here western country loses a damn good man when I cash in. Where's that doctor? Where's Tolman?"

"Who killed Buck Dennig?" asked Hashknife.

"I dunno. Think I'd let him live, if I knowed. Yo're Hartley, ain't yuh? I 'member you. Are you a damn detective?"

"Do I look like one?" smiled Hashknife.

"Why don'tcha go and arrest Tex Blanco, if yuh are?"

"Did Tex Blanco kill him, Luke?"

"I dunno. Gimme a drink, can'tcha? How bad does a man have to be hurt before he gets a drink? Where's that doctor? I'm bleedin' to death, I tell yuh."

"Listen to me, Luke," said Hashknife seriously. "What do yuh know about the killin' of Buck Dennig? What do yuh know about that ten thousand they stole from him?"

Luke blinked painfully. "I think Tolman knew," he said hoarsely. "They quarrelled the mornin' Buck drawed that money. I heard some of it. Tolman gambled for big money. Buck tried to stop him. I didn't hear it all, but I know Tolman said, 'We split here, Buck. I'll buy or sell. Ten thousand down and the rest on time.'

"That's what I heard that mornin'. Tolman knows, damn his dirty hide."

The doctor came elbowing his way through the crowd, and Hashknife got to his feet. That end of the room was packed solid with interested humanity, but

Tolman had vanished. Hashknife did not wait to hear the doctor's verdict, but went back to his horse.

He was no nearer a solution than he was before. But he knew now that Cleve Tolman and Buck Dennig had quarrelled, and that Tolman knew Buck was to draw that money. Evidently Buck had decided to buy out Tolman's interest in the TD, and had drawn the money to make the initial payment.

And it was also evident that old Luke Jones had tried to blackmail Tolman out of a thousand dollars, knowing that his evidence might convict Tolman. As far as the shooting was concerned, Tolman would have little trouble in proving self-defense, but he might have trouble in explaining away what old Luke had told about him.

But there were others things which Hashknife had discovered; little things which no one else had considered. He rode back to the B Arrow, and found only Mrs. Blanco and the doctor awake. The doctor assured Hashknife that all the patients were doing as well as might be expected; so Hashknife rode on to Pineville, knowing that all the beds were filled at the ranch.

CHAPTER TWELVE

There was a light in the sheriff's office. Hashknife tied his horse and knocked on the door. The sheriff, half-dressed, came to the door and glared icily at Hashknife.

"F'r God's sake, what are you doin' around here?" he demanded. "I hoped you wouldn't *never* come back."

"I saw a light," grinned Hashknife. "The rest of Pineville is fast asleep. Yo're up late, ain't yuh?"

"Aw, hell! C'mon in. I think I'd like to talk with you."

Hashknife followed him in and the sheriff shut the door. Oscar, the deputy, was stretched out on a cot, snoring stentoriously. The sheriff sat down at his desk and motioned Hashknife to a chair near him.

"Set down," he growled. "I swore to myself that I'd curry you with a six-gun if yuh ever came in here again."

"Oh, yuh never want to feel thataway about anybody, Sheriff."

"You made me so mad. What are yuh tryin' to do, anyway? Goin' down to the B Arrow and —"

"Keepin' you from gettin' Oscar's gun?"

"The big jug-head!"

"How does it come yo're up so late — or early?"

"Yuh don't know, eh? Well, I'll tell yuh why. Fifteen minutes ago Cleve Tolman left here. He was here for half an hour, and he told me about havin' to shoot Luke Jones."

"Yeah?" Hashknife smiled. "Tell yuh why he shot him?"

"Old Luke had been drinkin', kinda got loco and opined to kill Cleve, didn't he?"

"Did Tolman tell you I was there, Sheriff?"

"He said yuh was. You didn't see the shootin', didja?"

"Nope. Oh, I reckon he shot in self-defense."

"He said he did. Hartley" — the sheriff stretched wearily — "who shot yore pardner at the B Arrow?"

"Who knows?"

"Was it Tex Blanco?"

"I never thought of that."

"Did you shoot Tex Blanco?"

"I hope not."

"Mm-m-m-m. Was Luke Jones dead when you left Garnet?"

"Nope. I don't know how badly he was hurt."

"Why did you go from the B Arrow to Garnet?"

"Exercisin' my bronc."

"Oh, I see. I suppose you were just exercisin' yore bronc when yuh went out to the B Arrow."

"No, I went out there to keep you from makin' a fool of yourself."

"To keep me? Yo're crazy, Hartley, sometimes I like you. Yessir, I think yo're fine, when yuh mind yore own business; but right here and now I want to tell yuh to keep yore long nose out of my business. I can run my office."

"Then yuh don't need any help a-tall?" innocently.

"Yo're damn right, I don't!"

"You can catch'm all by yourself, eh?"

"All the catchin' I need — yes."

"You ought to run Scotland Yard."

"What's that?"

"Oh, a little corral they've got in London."

"I dunno anythin' about that, but I do sabe my own job."

"You must be a great help to the county."

The sheriff glowered at his sock-clad feet, and wiggled the big toe of his left foot, which protruded through a hole in the wool.

"I reckon I can get along without yore help," he said wearily.

"That's fine. Did Tolman tell yuh why he had to shoot Luke Jones?"

"He said Luke was loco, and imagined things. Wanted Cleve to pay him a thousand dollars, or he'd tell somethin'. Cleve said he didn't know what it was he was goin' to tell."

"Tolman didn't wait to see if Luke died."

"That don't mean anythin'. He shot in self-denfense."

"I suppose you'd like it fine if I'd go away and let yuh sleep, wouldn't yuh, Sheriff?"

"I sure would."

The sheriff didn't tell him good-bye, but he did slam the door rather hard, after Hashknife was outside. Hashknife laughed to himself, and went to the hotel.

Doctor Brent did not leave the B Arrow until morning. All of his patients were doing well, due to the fact that he had been on the spot to handle their wounds at once. Sleepy was in worse shape than any, but told the doctor if he saw Hashknife to tell him that everything was fine.

The doctor met Hashknife in front of the hotel and delivered the message. By this time nearly every one in Pineville knew of the shooting at the B Arrow, and many had heard of the shooting of Luke Jones at Garnet.

Hashknife was passing the post office, when Henry Goff, the postmaster, accosted him from the doorway.

"I've got a letter for you, Hartley," he said. "Sent to yuh in care of the sheriff, but he don't call for his mail until after the stage gets in this afternoon, and I thought it might be important."

Hashknife thanked him and went in to get the letter. It was in a plain envelope, slightly soiled, and the pencilled line inside read:

> "We got one of you, and your next. — THE BUNCH."

Hashknife compared it with the other letter he had from the Bunch, and it did not require a practiced eye to see that the messages had not been written by the same person. In fact, they were not alike in any detail. Hashknife smiled to himself and went down to the sheriff's office, where he found Oscar Johnson.

"Pat's gone out to the B Arrow," he told Hashknife. "The things that happened out there last night has got him kinda pawin' his head. He knowed you wasn't out there; so he went out. Said he might git at the bottom of things if you wasn't around to horn in and spoil the deal. My God, but he was mad about that six-shooter deal."

Hashknife showed Oscar the warning.

"By golly, they mean business, don't they?" exclaimed Oscar. "So it was the Bunch who shot Stevens and Tex. That lets Tex out, unless Tex —"

"Unless Tex what?"

"Well," said Oscar slowly, "Tex was out there and got mixed up in the shootin'."

"Did he do any shootin'?"

"I'll be darn if I know. He had my gun, yuh know; and I forgot to take it away from him when he came back in."

"So there's no way of connectin' Tex with the shootin'."

"Not a bit. Honest t' God," wailed Oscar. "There's a lot of things happenin' around here, and always there ain't no clue. Somethin' wipes out the evidence. Me and Pat are jist about disgusted."

"Were you awake when Cleve Tolman came here last night — or rather this mornin'?"

"Shore — partly. He shot Luke Jones in Garnet."

"I know all about that part of it; I was there."

"Oh, yeah; I think Pat mentioned it. He wondered what you was doin' there. Tolman said that old Luke was loco from too much drink. Demanded a thousand dollars from Tolman, and started to draw a gun on Tolman, when Tolman wouldn't give him the money. Old Luke has been makin' his own liquor at the TD, and that kinda stuff will make yuh crazy."

Hashknife did not tell Oscar what Luke Jones had said. He knew that the story would circulate fast enough, anyway. It was nearly noon when the sheriff came back from the B Arrow, and he was not in a pleasant frame of mind. Hashknife came down to his office and inquired about the sick and injured at the ranch.

"I didn't see 'em," growled the sheriff. "Old lady Blanco wouldn't let me in the house. Said the doctor gave her orders not to let anybody in to see 'em. But I saw Miss Evans, and I shore told her about that gun. She sent one of the punchers to Mrs. Cooper, with a note, askin' her why she told me what she did. And now, by God, I've got to apologize to Mrs. Cooper."

"She didn't confess, eh?"

"Hell, no! I lied to get a confession."

"Lyin' seems to be a popular pastime around here."

"Oh, go to hell!"

Hashknife laughed softly. "Pat Lynch, who do yuh think killed Buck Dennig?"

"I dunno. My gosh, if I knowed —"

"Who robbed the stage?"

"Tex Blanco."

"Who killed Shearer and robbed the bank?"

"I dunno."

"The only thing yo're sure of is that Tex Blanco robbed the stage, eh?"

"That's all."

"All right. Just for the sake of an argument; how often is money carried on that stage?"

The sheriff looked sharply at Hashknife. "Not very often, I'd say."

"Would Tex know enough about it to pick the right day?"

"Not unless he was told."

"Who could tell him — Windy March?"

"I'll bet he could."

"If the money was sent to Windy, he might."

"What are yuh drivin' at? Are you protectin' Tex Blanco? And what's all this talk about? What's all this to you? It seems to me that yo're takin' a lot of interest in all this stuff. Tex lost his gun after he held up that stage, and them women found it.

"If it hadn't been for Oscar, the Swede jug-head, we'd have Tex in jail. And if it hadn't been for you, we'd have had him, anyway. I could jail you for what you done."

"Yeah? And I could have made Stormy River County laugh you out of the state of Wyoming. Anyway" — seriously — "you always want to look before yuh leap, Sheriff. Look at this."

He let the sheriff read his latest warning.

"Tex never posted that," declared Hashknife. "He hasn't written a line since Sleepy got shot, and he couldn't have known that the Bunch was goin' to get one of us."

"You ought to be a detective, Hartley. Still, you wouldn't be much use, because yo're always goin' around provin' that everybody is innocent. Heffner's yellin' his head off for a chance to convict somebody. The county commissioner is ridin' him, and he's ridin' me. I'm ready to quit."

"You hadn't ought to do that, Sheriff. There's worse sheriffs than you are."

"Where?" asked Lynch bluntly.

"Well, I just can't answer yuh off-hand."

"That's supposed to be funny, ain't it?"

"It's all in yore point of view, Sheriff."

When the stage arrived that afternoon, Windy March brought the information that Luke Jones wasn't dead, and wasn't liable to die until his appointed time.

"Danged old wood rat wasn't hurt much," laughed Windy. "Swore he was dyin', they tell me. Had a pint of whisky in the inside pocket of his coat, and the bullet smashed it all to hell, cracked one of Luke's ribs and tunnelled under the skin plumb around to his back.

"The doctor dug the bullet out, tied a few yards of bandage around Luke and let him go. Luke was plenty sick, but he went back to the Overland Saloon and celebrated his resurrection by gettin' as drunk as a boiled owl. I seen him this mornin', settin' on the sidewalk, runnin' a rag through his six-gun, and singin' to himself."

As Windy was telling them about Luke Jones, Bud Hough drove through town in a buckboard, accompanied by a short, heavy-set man, dressed in black. Bud waved at the men around the stage, but the other man merely nodded.

"I wondered what Bud was doin' in Garnet," said Windy. "Must have been there to git that feller. I seen him git off the train."

"Prob'ly somebody visitin' Tolman," said Oscar.

CHAPTER THIRTEEN

Hashknife rode out to the B Arrow that afternoon, and found Sleepy getting along fine. Tex was around the house, bandaged and wearing his left arm in a sling. Little Jimmy's fever had been broken, and their greatest concern was to keep him quiet.

Sleepy didn't remember getting hit. He heard one shot fired, and remembered reaching for his gun. The rest of it was a complete blank. He was anxious to know what Hashknife had accomplished, but Hashknife was unable to tell him anything, except about the gun fight between Tolman and Luke Jones.

Hashknife did not tell him about the last warning, because it would only serve to worry Sleepy. He met Marion on the front porch, as he was leaving, and she told him that Mrs. Cooper had denied telling the sheriff about finding that gun.

"The sheriff told me," laughed Hashknife. "It was one way of gettin' you to confess, yuh see. It's been done many times. What are you goin' to do about provin' that Buck Dennig was yore brother?"

"I don't know. But that can wait. I asked the doctor not to mention it to any one, and I wish you would do the same."

"Shore; it's all right with me."

Marion stood with her hands on the rail, staring off across the hills.

"Just to think that Blaine came away out here, hiding from the world, and made a success. And that Fate sent me out here too — but too late to find him. Do you believe in Fate, Mr. Hartley?"

"Yes'm."

"Did Fate send you here to help us — me, I mean?"

"Yuh might say she did, Miss Evans; Fate and necessity."

"Necessity?"

"We needed the money, I reckon."

"But why would anybody wish to kill you and Mr. Stevens?"

"Well," smiled Hashknife, "I reckon they believe in Fate, too; and they're afraid the cards fall wrong, with us in the game."

"Do you believe Tex Blanco robbed that stage?"

"Do you, Miss Evans?"

"I did."

"So did I."

"The sheriff believes he did, Mr. Hartley. Oh, I suppose many other folks believe he did; and how in the world can he ever prove his innocence?"

"They can't prove his guilt, Miss Evans."

"Would you want to go through life that way?"

"It is kinda tough. I can see his point of view. No jury on earth would believe his story of what happened to him the night before the robbery. I believe him, even if it does sound fishy. I shore hope that some day — Miss Evans, you kinda like Tex Blanco, don'tcha?"

Marion turned away and walked to the end of the porch.

"Aw, shucks!" grunted Hashknife. "I wasn't tryin' to act smart and pry into yore affairs. I'm no blind man. And love ain't nothin' to make fun about. Don't get sore about it and put groundglass in Sleepy's mush."

Marion was laughing, and Hashknife crossed the porch to her.

"You ain't sore at me? Gee, that's great. Are you goin' to marry Tex Blanco?"

Marion shook her head slowly.

"Gee, that's great!"

Marion turned quickly and she was not laughing now.

"What is great about it?"

"To think that a pretty girl really has sense. I shore was scared you was goin' to marry him."

"What is that to you?" she asked, her eyes snapping.

"Nothin' to me, of course, except that I don't like to see a pretty girl throw herself away on a man with a reputation like he's got. Tex is virtually an outlaw. He's just out of jail, because they can't put the deadwood on him. They all know he's guilty, but they can't prove it.

"You couldn't marry a man like him, Miss Evans. You'd ruin yore life. When they told me yuh was liable to marry him I didn't believe it. I got one look at yuh and I said you had too many brains for a thing like that. I'm glad I'm right. It ain't often I'm mistaken in human nature."

"Thank you," she said icily, turning to the door. "I'm inclined to agree with the sheriff, when he says that you have a nasty habit of meddling in affairs which do not belong to you."

She closed the door behind her, leaving Hashknife alone on the porch. He leaned against a porch post, a twinkle in his gray eyes, the corner of his wide mouth twisting to a grin. He went slowly down to the ground and walked to his horse.

Tex came striding out through the kitchen and halted Hashknife. It was not difficult for Hashknife to see that Tex was mad. He came up to Hashknife, who was standing beside his gray horse.

"What did you say to Miss Evans, Hartley?" he demanded.

"Why, I dunno," innocently. "What did she say?"

"She didn't say anythin', but I know you did, because she was cryin'. Lemme tell you somethin', Hartley; you —"

"You didn't ask her if she was mad, didja?"

"She was cryin', I tell yuh."

"Sometimes folks cry when they're glad, Blanco."

Tex glanced back toward the house.

"Glad?" He turned and looked at Hashknife. "What has she got to be glad over?"

"I dunno, I'm sure. Yuh might ask her?"

"Yeah, I might."

"Does yore shoulder hurt, Blanco?"

"Not very much. I can stand the pain all right. You didn't hurt her feelin's, did yuh?"

"I tried to be easy. Blanco, did you ask her to marry you?"

"I did not," firmly.

"Why don'tcha?"

"I'm no fool, Hartley. How could a man in my position ask a girl to marry him? She'd be a fool to marry me."

"That's what I told her — and she got mad at me."

"You — uh —" Tex opened and shut his mouth several times, while Hashknife swung easily to his saddle.

"You'd be a fool to ask her, and she'd be a fool to accept," said Hashknife, gathering up his reins. "But go ahead. If men and women didn't marry because they knew they were fools, we'd run out of population in a little while."

"Well," said Tex slowly, "you — I don't sabe you. This is none of your business."

"I know it," seriously. "But if I minded my own business, you'd have a lot of misery ahead of yuh."

Hashknife reined his horse around and galloped down through the big gate, leaving Tex to wonder what he meant. He watched Hashknife ride away, and wandered around to the front porch, where he found Marion alone. She was seated in an old rocker, a magazine in her lap.

He sat down on the top step of the porch.

"Has Mr. Hartley gone?" asked Marion.

"Yeah, he's gone," said Tex. "What did he say that made you cry, Marion?"

She did not answer him, and he finally turned to look at her.

"He said you'd be a fool to marry me, didn't he, Marion?"

Marion looked down at the magazine. "Yes," she said softly.

"He told me he did," said Tex.

"He told you? What did you say, Tex?"

"I agreed with him."

"Oh."

"What else could I do, Marion?"

"I — I didn't know that the question had ever come up," she said slowly. "It made me mad to have some one suggest that I would be a fool to do something I had never really considered doing."

"That's what made me mad, too," said Tex. "I — I knew you would never be able to marry me. Gosh, I'm no fool. Mebby I was a fool a while ago; but I didn't stop to think. I wish Hartley would stay away and mind his own business."

"I do too, Tex."

"Well, if you say so, I'll see that he does."

"I suppose he'll have to come out here to see his partner."

"We'll have him moved to town."

"The doctor says he must stay here here until that heals."

Tex hammered his heel against the step savagely.

"Well, there's nothin' to be done. Anyway, we can keep away from him while he's here."

"Certainly. Still, that is poor thanks for what he did, Tex. If it hadn't been for him, you would be in jail now."

"That's true," grudgingly. "Why did he do it, Marion?"

Marion shook her head. "I asked Sleepy, and he said it was because Hashknife couldn't help doing things like that. He says that Hashknife never did any one a wrong in his life. I don't know what Sleepy's idea of wrong and right amounts to, of course. I reminded him that Hashknife lied to Hootie Cooper about knowing Hootie's brother, and he said, 'Miss Evans, you can find lies in the Bible, if you look close enough; and Hashknife's lie didn't hurt anybody'."

"No, I don't reckon it did, Marion. Well, here comes the doctor. He's shore a faithful person."

The next two days were uneventful. Hashknife made daily trips to the B Arrow, but he did not travel the road. The doctor said that Sleepy would be able to travel in about another week. Tex's wound was healing nicely, and Jimmy Hastings was out of danger. Hashknife had a long talk with John Rice, the banker, regarding Buck Dennig. The bank had opened its doors again, but Rice told Hashknife that Tolman had resigned as a director.

Old Luke Jones came back to Pineville, still half-drunk; more grouchy than ever. He refused to talk with Hashknife about the things he had blurted out in Garnet, when he thought he was bleeding to death. A few stitches in his side caused him to walk with a decided list, but outside of that he was as good as new.

Hashknife had not seen Tolman since the shooting at Garnet, but the rest of the outfit had been to town. He had talked with Shorty Gallup about Buck Dennig, and he mentioned the things old Luke had spoken about.

"Old Luke better look out for Tolman," said Shorty.

"He talked as though Tolman knew somethin' about the killin' of Dennig," said Hashknife.

"I dunno," said Shorty vaguely. "I think he's crazy about Buck havin' any relatives. Still, yuh never can tell. Luke and Buck were good friends, and Buck might have told him more than he told us."

"What's yore honest opinion on who killed Dennig?"

"I wouldn't even make a guess."

"It must have been somebody that knew Buck had that ten thousand dollars, don't yuh think?"

"Mebby. Buck always carried quite a roll. Somebody might have killed him for what he carried, picked up that big roll and didn't wait to grab that hundred and sixty he had in another pocket."

"Yeah, that's true. Probably the same gang robbed the stage."

"Looks thataway. What a cinch they had. That sheriff and deputy couldn't foller a load of hay in the snow. What we need is a good detective."

"Had one, didn't they?"

"I reckon so. Didn't last long. Any detective is a fool to come in openly on a case like this, don'tcha know it?"

"I suppose yo're right, Gallup. What do yuh think about Tex Blanco?"

"Oh, Tex is all right, I reckon. Anyway, he's slick; I'll say that much for him."

"Slick?"

"Shore. They can't pin anythin' on him, can they? I'll say they can't. How's yore pardner gettin' along?"

"Be out in a week."

"Got any idea who shot him?"

"Yeah," said Hashknife seriously.

Shorty eyed him closely. "Do yuh mean that, Hartley?"

"I think I know."

"That sounds interestin'. Why don'tcha do somethin'?"

"Can't do a thing, until I'm sure."

"Why did they shoot him?"

Hashknife laughed softly. "They thought poor old Sleepy was a detective. He don't know yet why they shot him, and I don't want to tell him, 'cause he might pull out some of his stitches, laughin'."

"Oh," said Shorty dryly. "That's why they shot him, eh?"

"Sure. We've been warned to get out of the country."

"Yuh did? Well, I'll be darned. That detective was warned too, wasn't he? Can yuh imagine that. They think yo're workin' for the Cattle Association, eh?"

"They didn't say who we was workin' for. I dunno where they got the idea, I'm sure."

"Well, ain't yuh scared to stay around here, Hartley?"

"I'm still here, ain't I? Sure I'm scared. When men shoot at yuh in the dark, it pays to be scared."

"Yo're danged right. Well, I've got to be headin' for the ranch. See yuh later, Hartley."

"So long, Gallup."

The following morning Hashknife went to the B Arrow with the doctor, feeling sure that no one would molest them together. Sleepy wanted to get out of bed, but the doctor warned him against it.

After the doctor had gone back to town, Tex asked Hashknife if he would stay at the ranch for a while. Marion wanted to go to town, it seemed, and Tex also wanted to go. But Tex was unable to handle the team with one hand; so Frank Judd was elected to drive. Tex didn't want to leave his mother alone with the two patients; so Hashknife agreed to stay.

It was about an hour later, while Hashknife was enjoying a siesta on the front porch, that Bud Hough and Dobe Severn, from the TD outfit, came past, heading toward Garnet. Hashknife waved at them and they drew up at the gate, while he walked down to them.

He noticed that both men had war bags fastened to their saddles, and this meant that they were travelling away.

"Pullin' out?" he asked.

"Goin' down to the XOX outfit, south of Wallgate," said Bud. "Change of pasture makes fat calves, yuh know," laughing. "Same man owns both ranches."

"You mean the same man owns the XOX and the TD?"

"Shore. Name's Billings. Ed Billings."

"I thought Tolman owned the TD."

"Sellin' out today."

"Is that so?" Hashknife was thinking swiftly. "Today, eh? Kinda quick sale, ain't it?"

"Billings has been out there with us for two or three days. They been dickerin' for a week or so. Heffner, the lawyer is handlin' the deal."

"Is he goin' to keep the rest of the crew?"

"I think all but Shorty and Sturgis. They might stay, but Matt said they might go with Tolman. Well, we'll drift on. If yuh want a job, yuh better strike Billings right away."

Hashknife hurried back to the house and met Mrs. Blanco at the steps.

"I've got to go," he told her, and ran for his horse.

In town old Luke Jones, like a sore-headed bear, was looking for trouble. Everybody ignored him, because he was dangerous, and being ignored was something old Luke hated.

"You better cool off," advised the sheriff. "Somebody is liable to bust yore earthly envelope, if yuh don't look out, Jones. You ain't sober enough to make a fight."

"Zasso?" Old Luke shoved out his lean jaw at Pat Lynch.

"Show me somebody that wants to choose me, Pat. I'm here to be selected by anybody on earth — pre — pref-er-bly Cleve Tolman. He's my meat, the dirty sidewinder."

"Aw, go sleep it off," advised the sheriff, and walked away.

He had tried to start an argument with Bud Hough and Dobe Severn, but they had ridden along, ignoring him. Shorty, Matt and Alex dodged him for half an hour, with Alex arguing all the time with Shorty, to keep him from going back and accepting Luke's challenge.

Fortunately Luke did not see Tolman and Billings arrive and go to the court house. Heffner was busy with a civil case, and they were obliged to wait until he finished; so they waited in his office.

Tex, Marion and Judd arrived, tied their horses in front of Hootie Cooper's store and went in to see him. Mrs. Cooper was there, and she chuckled with glee over Marion.

"The school teacher was a frost," Mrs. Cooper declared. "He whipped both of the Beebee kids the second day, and sent Ella Hall home with a note, askin' her folks to teach her not to carry tales. Oh, he's still there, 'cause they've got to have a teacher, but old Sam and Beebee asked me how soon you was comin' back."

Marion laughed, but shook her head. "I don't think I could take the school again, Ma Cooper."

Mrs. Cooper looked sideways at Tex and nodded sagely.

"You've had an awful time out there, ain't yuh, Marion?"

"But I've enjoyed it."

"*You* would. Oh, don't hope me. I don't blame yuh. I shore was surprised at yore note about that gun. Pat Lynch shore lied, didn't he. And he's dodged me ever since. But he told Hootie what happened. You ought to love Hashknife Hartley, even if he is a liar. C'mon over to the house and let's talk."

"All right, Ma."

Marion walked over to Tex and told him she was going home with Mrs. Cooper for a few minutes.

"That's fine," he told her. "Don't hurry."

They had just opened the door, when Hashknife's tall gray fairly spiked his tail against the sidewalk, throwing gravel all over them. He was off the horse and up to them before they recovered.

"C'mon with me, Miss Evans!" he panted. "Don't ask questions, 'cause we might be too late."

Tex and Frank Judd ran out of the store, wondering what it was all about, and they saw Hashknife hurrying down the sidewalk, holding Marion by the elbow.

"What's the idea?" asked Tex wonderingly.

"That's what I want to know," said Mrs. Cooper. "That tall cowboy is shore sudden. They're goin' into the court house."

"Well, I'm goin' to find out," growled Tex, and hurried down the street with Judd.

CHAPTER FOURTEEN

Hashknife did not bother to tell Marion what it was all about, as he rushed her up the one flight of stairs and down the hall to Heffner's office. He opened the door and shoved her in ahead of him.

Tolman and Billings were seated at a table, while Heffner was standing up, enumerating something from a legal-looking paper. All three men turned quickly at the interruption.

"I am engaged just at present," said Heffner quickly. If you will wait a few minutes, I will be at your service."

"I reckon this is the right time," said Hashknife. He was out of breath and snapped his words sharply.

Tolman started to his feet, a scowl on his face, as Hashknife came closer to the table.

"Ain't been no deed signed yet, has there?" asked Hashknife.

"Why — not yet," faltered Heffner. "I don't see —"

"Then there won't be none signed, folks. I understand that Mr. Tolman is sellin' the TD — all of the TD, and it just happens that this lady is Miss Marion Evans, sisters to Blaine Evans, deceased, who was known to you as Buck Dennig."

For a moment there was silence, as all three men stared at Marion. Then Tolman laughed shortly.

"What kind of a hold-up game is this?" he asked harshly.

"Not any hold-up, Tolman. Miss Evans can prove it. You've no right to sell all the ranch. In fact, I don't reckon you've got any right to sell any of it, until an accountin' has been made."

"Why, this claim is ridiculous."

"Ask Luke Jones, Tolman."

"That old liar!"

"You shot him, yuh know."

"I shot him because he tried to shoot me."

"Why did he want to shoot yuh, Tolman?"

"He's crazy."

"That's a weak answer. Anyway, there won't be no sale — not now, Heffner."

"I guess not," replied the attorney. "If you had been ten minutes later, it would have required a lot of legal red tape to settle the matter."

Tolman jerked his hat down over his eyes and walked from the room.

Tex and Judd had stopped just outside the doorway, listening to what was being sad, but Tolman did not look at them as he went past.

"I'm sorry about this," said Billings. "Of course, you understand I knew nothing about it."

"You couldn't know, Mr. Billings," agreed Heffner warmly.

"I suppose it saves me a lot of time and money, as long as it had to happen. Miss Evans" — he held out his hand to Marion — "if you ever want to sell your half of the TD, just write me in care of the XOX Ranch, at Wallgate."

"Thank you," said Marion weakly. "I — I don't know what it is all about yet myself."

Hashknife grinned at her. "Go ahead and howl me out for not mindin' my own business."

"But how did you know?" asked Tex. "How on earth did you know this sale was being made here?"

"Couple little birds rode past and told me, Tex. You can talk it over with Mr. Heffner, or" — Hashknife pointed toward the open door — "down the hall a couple doors is where they issue marriage licenses."

He laughed and walked from the room.

Tolman had halted at the sidewalk, seething with anger. He knew Marion was Buck's sister; knew it before anybody else did. But he took a chance on disposing of the TD, hoping to get away before anybody discovered the fact, if they ever did. He blamed old Luke Jones, although he wondered how old Luke found out who Marion was. Tolman knew that Marion and Buck looked alike; he had seen that the first time he met her, and wondered why others didn't see it too.

Tolman didn't want to make an accounting of what he had done with Buck's share of the ranch, and he stood there on the edge of the sidewalk, trying to figure out his next move.

Suddenly old Luke Jones lurched out of the Stormy River saloon and started across the street. Tolman forgot his troubles, when he saw his old ex-cook. He stepped into the street and started toward old Luke, who stopped short.

"Go back to yore hole, you dirty old badger!" rasped Tolman.

Old Luke laughed. Hashknife stepped out to the sidewalk, and saw them walking toward each other. Old Luke had both hands in the pockets of his frayed coat, and he did not take them out. He was not wearing a holstered gun. Hashknife stepped out of line with them. Some one was running up the sidewalk, and Hashknife turned to see the sheriff.

"Stop it, Tolman!" he yelled. But Tolman didn't stop. They were not over ten feet apart when Tolman jerked out his gun, and at the same instant the side of Luke's coat seemed to erupt a cloud of smoke.

Tolman jerked sideways, half-turned, tried to recover his balance, but couldn't do it; so he staggered back on his heels and went sprawling in the street, still clutching his big Colt gun.

"Oh, God!" panted the sheriff. "Got him cold."

Old Luke pounded the fire out of his coat, as he looked at Tolman, flat on his back in the street. Men were running from every direction. Shorty Gallup was the first to reach old Luke, and flung both arms around him.

"Somebody git a rope!" yelled Shorty. "Git a rope!"

"No yuh don't!" snorted the sheriff. "I saw it myself. I don't like old Luke no better than you do, but give the devil his dues. Luke shot in self-defense."

"Lemme alone!" growled Luke. "Git yore paws off me, Gallup, or I'll pistol-whip yuh."

Hashknife looked back toward the entrance to the court house. Tex and Judd were coming across the street, while Marion had joined Mrs. Cooper and several more people in front of the store.

The sheriff and Hashknife made a quick examination of Tolman. It did not require a lengthy examination. The sheriff got to his feet and looked at old Luke.

"You made a complete job of it, Luke," he said coldly.

"He had it comin', Pat." Old Luke looked around at the crowd, which had gathered in the street. "I'll bet yuh ten dollars that Cleve Tolman killed Buck Dennig. Anybody want to take that bet?"

"If I take yore bet, can yuh prove it?" asked Hashknife.

Luke shut one eye and looked at Hashknife.

"I can come nearer provin' that Tolman killed him than anybody else that Tex Blanco killed him."

The eyes of the crowd shifted to Tex. Oscar Johnson had joined the crowd, and was standing beside the sheriff. Old Luke laughed gratingly, and began talking again. Hashknife whispered softly to the sheriff:

"Back my play, Pat. It'll come quick now. Tell Oscar."

The sheriff drew a quick breath, shot a quick glance at Hashknife, but spoke softly to Oscar, who looked at him in a blank sort of a way.

"I tell yuh, I'll bet ten dollars," reiterated Luke.

"Somebody bet him," laughed Hashknife, and stepped over beside Shorty Gallup. "You bet him, Shorty."

"Why should I bet him?" growled Shorty.

"Mebby yore pardner, Sturgis, will take the bet?"
Sturgis shot a quick glance at Hashknife.
"I ain't got no money to bet," growled Matt Sturgis.
"What didja do with all yuh got?" asked Hashknife, and his voice fairly snapped.
"What do yuh mean?" Sturgis whirled, facing Hashknife. "What's all this about. What money?"
Sturgis swung his hand over the butt of his gun, eyes snapping.
Hashknife was covered by the body of Shorty Gallup; so he had little fear of Matt's gun. And Shorty did not seem able to move. Hashknife glanced at the sheriff, who had his gun in his hand, a queer expression in his face, as he tried to puzzle things out.
"Shorty," said Hashknife, "which one of you two are goin' to confess first?"
That sentence was like an electric shock to Shorty. He ducked sideways, jerking at his gun, but it was not there, because Hashknife had deftly plucked it out with his left hand, just before Shorty ducked.
Matt Sturgis did not shoot; did not even draw a gun. He started to back away, thinking to escape, but the sheriff and deputy had him covered. He backed about six steps, before he threw up both hands in token of surrender.
"I quit," he choked. "My God! I'll talk," he blubbered, as the sheriff stepped over and took his gun.
"Talk, you dirty quitter!" rasped Shorty. He had both hands above his shoulders, and was looking at the muzzle of Hashknife's gun. "Go ahead and talk yourself into a rope."

"You two killed Buck Dennig, robbed the stage and killed Guy Shearer," said Hashknife.

"Shorty killed Buck," declared Matt. He was almost crying.

"Gimme a gun," begged Shorty. "Lemme kill him, won't yuh? I swear to give it back as soon as I kill him. He's yaller as mustard."

"Sturgis, stop blubberin'," ordered Hashknife. "Shearer forged that ten thousand dollar cheque, didn't he?"

"Uh-huh. Buck and Tolman quarrelled and Shorty heard 'em. We framed with Shearer for a three-way split, and he forged Buck's signature. Shorty killed Buck, and we hid the money."

"Yes, and damn you, you killed Shearer!" roared Shorty.

Sturgis was on the verge of collapse.

"Better lock 'em up, sheriff," said Hashknife. "They've told enough."

Both men went willingly, and some of the crowd carried Tolman's body into the saloon. Heffner had reached there in time to hear part of the confession. Tex seemed dazed, unable to comprehend what it was all about. Hashknife slapped him on the shoulder and Tex jerked out of his trance.

"That clears you, Tex," he said softly. "If I was you I'd go across the street and talk to a certain lady. She might want to know about it, don'tcha think?"

Tex blinked at Hashknife, turned and walked slowly toward the crowd on the opposite sidewalk, where Judd was telling them what it was all about.

Hashknife and Heffner walked into the saloon, where most of the crowd were gathered, and in a few moments the sheriff came in. McLean was the only one left of the TD outfit, and he looked frightened to death. He came straight to Hashknife.

"I — I didn't have anythin' to do with it, Hartley," he said.

"I had you on my list for a while," grinned Hashknife.

"My God, I'm glad yuh marked me off."

Hashknife laughed. "It was lucky for me that Shorty and Sturgis caved in. I wasn't sure of Sturgis, but I had a big hunch, because they were together a lot, and Sturgis was related to Shearer. I knew Shearer was in on it, as soon as I studied that cheque. The signature was clever, but he didn't follow it out in writing all the cheque.

"The warnin' they sent to Sears, the detective, was written by Shearer. He also wrote the first one to me and my pardner. But the last one I got was written by some one else, because Shearer was dead. I think they were goin' to rob the bank vault, with the help of Shearer, and intended merely ropin' him up to make it look good; but they got greedy and killed him, for fear he'd talk, or to make their shares bigger.

"They stole a rope from the B Arrow, cut the hondoo off and left it on the floor to convict Tex Blanco. But the key that unlocked the inside door of that vault was on Shearer's key ring in Shearer's pocket. If they had forced him to unlock that door, they'd never let him put his hand in his pocket afterwards.

"Shearer told 'em about the money comin' on the stage. I ain't sure just what their idea was, but I figure they went to the B Arrow to pick up somethin' to incriminate Tex Blanco, and get a chance that night to knock out Tex and kidnap him. Anyway, they left his gun at the scene of the holdup, and Miss Evans and Mrs. Cooper found it.

"That's shore the truth," agreed the sheriff warmly. "Oscar dumped Miss Evans' trunk in the river, and when he tried to dry out the things he found the gun. Like a darn jug-head, he traded handles, and killed the evidence."

The crowd laughed.

"And Tex knew that no jury would believe his story; so he never told it," said Hashknife. "I talked with Shorty yesterday and he told me what he thought about the killin' of Buck Dennig. He said that somebody must have killed Buck for what little money he had, but found the big roll and overlooked the rest of it. Shorty and Matt tried hard to kill me and my pardner, and they almost got my pardner. I reckon that's all the story, unless Shorty and Matt know more than I do."

"I'll be damned if I believe it!" snorted the sheriff. "And I thought you was just a nosey damn puncher, who wasn't able to mind yore own business."

"What is your business, Hartley?" said Heffner.

"Me?" Hashknife laughed softly. "I'm the detective you sent for to the Cattle Association."

"You are? But Sears said —"

"Sears is a clerk. He had his orders to run at the first sign of trouble — and he did. I'll bet he's scared yet."

"And that's why yuh lied about where yuh come from!" exclaimed McLean.

"Yeah — and you come darn near gettin' me killed off by makin' me out a liar," laughed Hashknife. "You folks wasn't near as wise as Shorty was. But you didn't have a guilty conscience."

Hashknife left the saloon and went back to his horse. Marion, Tex, Mrs. Cooper, Hootie and Judd were there waiting for him. They had managed to understand what it was all about. He looked at them and his face wrinkled to a grin.

"Well, it was a nice afternoon, wasn't it?" he queried.

Mrs. Cooper came up to him, her fat face grinning with delight, and held out her hand to him.

"I want to be the first to shake hands with you," she said. "The rest of them just stand around and say, 'My God!' Tex Blanco has said it a dozen times already, and Hootie ain't far behind him. Marion ain't said much, but I'll bet she's thought a lot. Didja ever realize that she owns the TD outfit right now. Tolman ain't got a livin' relative."

Hashknife looked at Marion. Her face was white, and she was clinging to Tex's good arm, as though afraid he might get away from her.

Slowly Hashknife untied his horse and climbed into the saddle.

"It's funny what changes yuh can bring into the lives of folks, when yuh don't mind yore own business," he said slowly. "Sometimes I'm glad I'm nosey thataway. Well, I've got to get back and help Ma Blanco take care of the sick folks. Gotta get my pardner back on his feet, yuh see. There ain't nobody's business around here that looks worth my time mindin' it now. I'll see yuh later, folks."

He started to ride away, but stopped and called to Frank Judd. They talked for a moment, and then Hashknife rode on down the street.

Judd came back, a half-smile on his lips. They were watching Hashknife going down the street, sitting very straight in his saddle.

Tex sighed deeply. "Well, he must think I'm a fool. Honest to gosh, I couldn't talk to him. I wonder if he realizes what this means to me? Why, my God, I've got the weight of the world off my neck."

"Cleared with one swipe," said Hootie. "The long-legged son of a gun! I don't give a damn if he never was in Mizpa, Arizona, or never heard of my brother.

Whooee-e-e! Well, Ma" — he turned to Mrs. Cooper — "I reckon I better turn merchant again."

Old man Beebee was hurrying up the street, and caught sight of the group near the store. He came over to them, chewing violently.

"I jist heard about it!" he panted. "Missed it, of course. Always miss the fun of anythin', 'cause I had to wash the danged dishes. Oh, hallo, Miss Evans. Sa-a-ay! I reckon you can have that school any time yuh want it. Ma and Mrs. Hall have hauled in their horns, and the men folks are runnin' things again."

"She's all through teachin' school," said Tex.

"Oh! Well, I don't blame her. Awful job. Sorry."

He turned and headed for the Stormy River saloon.

Tex turned to Marion. "I guess we better go home, Marion."

"Yes," she said softly.

"You tell Mrs. Blanco I'll be out in a day or two," said Mrs. Cooper. "Mebby tomorrow."

"All right, Ma; we'll look for you."

They walked down to the buckboard, and got in, while Judd untied the team and handed the lines to Tex.

"I'm not goin' back with yuh, Tex," he said.

"Yo're not?"

"Nope. You can drive with one hand, can'tcha, Tex?"

Tex looked straight at Judd, who colored slightly.

"Why ain't you goin' with us, Frank?" he asked.

"Well, if yuh want to know so bad — Hashknife told me if I didn't let yuh come home alone, he'd whip hell out of me when we got there. And that jigger means what he says."

"Oh!" grunted Tex, gathering up the lines. "Well, under the circumstances, Frank, it's all right. Giddap, broncs."

"They walk if yuh let 'em," laughed Frank.

Tex nodded, and they went down the street and out on the winding road toward home.